Realia

Realia

Will Aitken

RANDOM HOUSE CANADA

Random House and colophon are trademarks.

Canadian Cataloguing in Publication Data

Aitken, Will
  Realia

ISBN 0-679-31040-1

I. Title.

PS8551.I78R42 2000   C813'.54   C99-933057-8
PR9199.3.A47R42 2000

Jacket design: Jonathan Howells
Text design: Sharon Foster Design

Printed and bound in the United States of America

First Edition

10 9 8 7 6 5 4 3 2 1

This book is for Susanne and Alexander Greenhalgh,
and Graham Callan and Robin Wilson,
inhabitants of another small island nation

Empty sister, eat to the full!

MOTTO ON A JAPANESE PENCIL BOX

Contents

Eurydice

Fair Eurydice, a wood nymph, was wife to Orpheus, a
princely singer whose voice was so sweet that wild beasts
lay down to his songs and trees and flowers bent to his
rhythms. They lived in Thrace, on the flanks of Mount Olympus.
One day Eurydice, bathing in the river with her friends the water
nymphs, was bitten by a serpent and died. Orpheus grieved for her
until his tears floated him down to the underworld where, with his
magic lyre, he persuaded the dark ones to allow his wife to return with
him to the light of day. They agreed to his request, but with one con-
dition: when he led Eurydice out of hell he should not look back on
her till they had gained the threshold of the world. Winged Hermes,
messenger to the gods, would accompany Eurydice on her return voy-
age. The road back was long, Orpheus's desire impetuous: he turned
to look, Eurydice died a second death. Hermes led her back down.

Doubly bereft, Orpheus lost himself in drink and song. It was
said that he wanted nothing more to do with women and surrounded
himself with comely youths. They met at night in a sealed house to

study the sacred mysteries the poet had brought back from the under-world. The women of Thrace, angry at their exclusion from house, mysteries, music and poetry, ambushed Orpheus and dismembered him. They threw the pieces into the river where Eurydice had died. His severed head, riding the current, sang its way down to the sea.

1

Everyone at Akasaka Pearl Hotel speak English.
No problem. Right away. I rush along gently curving corridors. Where do they keep the fucking ice
machine? Maids step behind their carts and bow as
I pass. Something like "Ohio" springs joyously to
their lips. "Ohio," I call back, feeling like an extra
in a Rodgers and Hammerstein musical. Part of
each floor—to the left of the elevators—seems set aside for
people like me. Not Westerners necessarily, but people who
dress like Westerners. As far as I can determine I am the
only Westerner at Akasaka Pearl, which everyone affects
not to notice. I return the favor. I would like, however,
some ice. I know it's seven a.m., but not on my time goddammit. A big plastic barrel of ice for the bottle of cognac
I picked up at duty-free.

I like it iced.

The bronze elevator doors open. A bellhop strides out,
straightening his pillbox cap. "Ice," I call out to him. "Ice!" he

smiles, bows, heads off down the corridor. I trot along at
his heels, the ice machine surely but yards away. Halfway
down the hall he knocks at a door. Ice. It swings open. A
man in a blue-and-white robe hands out a pair of black
wingtips. Door closes, bellhop bows to dark wood, turns
around to discover me staring down at him. "Ice," he assures
me. Bowing low he hurries off.

Back in my room I ring room service. "Ohio," a woman
answers.

"Ohio. You speak English?"

"Judamoma please."

On hold. Synthesizer version of "Home on the Range."

"How may I help you?" A man this time, we're moving
up the pecking order.

Explain my simple needs.

"Only ice?"

"Only ice."

"Ah." Strange watery intake of air. "Would you mind
holding?"

"Home, home on the range."

"How may I help you?" Different man. I think. Or part
of an elaborate game played with foreigners.

"I would like some ice please."

"And what else?"

"Nothing else. Just a big bucket of ice. You do have ice?"

"I will send it right up."

"Thank you so much."

I study the small green pamphlet on the dressing table:
WHAT TO DO IN CASE OF POTENTIAL DISASTER.
Earthquake instructions. Forgot they have those here. This

explains the heavy chrome flashlight in the dressing-table drawer and possibly the two identical bound volumes, one with the English title *The Teachings of Buddha*.

Knock at door. Same bellboy. Probably. He holds a silver salver set with a finger bowl full of ice and two bottles of club soda.

Formal presentation of bill.

I stare dumbly at four digits preceded by a yen sign. As far as I can calculate they're asking me to pay $24 for two bottles of fizzy water and a midget's handful of ice.

"I didn't order club soda."

The bellboy slides closer to me, keeping the salver between us. "Ice," he smiles.

Point to each frosty bottle and shake my head vehemently. "No club soda."

"You must."

The silver bottle caps catch the morning light. "I must?"

"For ice"—narrow index finger indicates the bowl— "you must order drink."

"Ah." With proffered pen I scribble at the bottom of the bill.

He places the tray on the dressing table and heads for the door.

"Just a moment." I press a 500-yen coin into his hand.

He studies his upturned palm, hands the coin back. "No tip."

Sit down on the bed, cool bottles sparkling on the tray before me. I pop one open and glug it down. Such pleasure courses through me. Away at last.

—

The man behind the long green glass desk at the Miyako Employment Agency tries to concentrate on the questionnaire in front of him but his attention keeps straying to an oddly shaped paperweight next to his in-tray. My eyes slide toward it as well. Looks too light to be a paperweight. Could be made of metal, plastic, stone. Deep sooty gray, glows like an opal.

He notices I'm staring. "Smoke?"

One of the questions on the form, I assume. "Occasionally," I reply, with a post-coital flash of teeth and gums to suggest which occasion. He doesn't get it. Or doesn't seem to. Both Mr. Okudas, the upright one and the other ripply hanging-upside-down fellow in the green glass surface of his desk, are perfectly opaque. Good English, but illegible.

He picks up the paperweight. Opens like a clamshell. "Mild Seven?"

Laugh harder than I meant to. "I thought it was a paperweight."

He smiles. Tiny teeth with minute spaces between. Wonder what can get caught in there.

"It's beautiful."

He shuts the case before I can select a fag and propels it across the glass to me.

Fits the palm of my hand like a flat cool egg. Still can't tell what it's made of. Hand it back. "I've never seen anything like it."

"A present from my wife. She has very good taste." I'm sure. Then something odd happens. For the next minute or so we sit and stare at the cigarette case, neither of us saying a word.

The spell breaks, he opens the case, I choose a fag, he takes one too. A shining pale globe appears in his hand. He extends it across the desk, fires me up.

"Very many Americans come to Japan now."

"I'm from Canada."

"Ah, Canada." I have said a magic word. He throws out his arms—"Canada is very wide"—then brings his hands together as if to applaud though his palms don't quite touch—"Japan very narrow."

I laugh appreciatively. Must we talk about Canada? I left my No-Doz in my other purse.

"What part?"

Huh?

"Of Canada?"

"Alberta."

If he weren't seated he'd be dancing about the room. "Canadian Rockies—they are so high!"

Aren't they. You can see them from Lethbridge. All you can see from Lethbridge, you want to talk *narrow*. "You've visited the Rockies?"

"Honeymoon. Five … six years ago. Banff, Lake Louise, Jasper. The nature. You are so lucky to come from there."

Who could resist all that nature? "Not a lot of theater in the Rockies."

He looks down at the forgotten questionnaire. Deep sigh followed by moist inrush of air through the tiny spaces between his teeth. "You wish to stay in Tokyo?"

"Tokyo is very nice. I'm just not sure I want to live in a big city."

He chuckles. "No nature."

"Kyoto sounds interesting."

"Kyoto!" Second magic word. "I am from Kyoto."

I find myself bowing in joyous acknowledgment of this fact.

"You know what they say about people from Kyoto?"

Do tell.

"Tokyo people are a little cold, work-work-work, fast-fast-fast. Kyoto people spicy, like their food. Kyoto people like to take it slow."

"Sounds like the place for me."

For a moment I catch him looking into my eyes. "But theater, in English—very difficult."

"It doesn't have to be theater—that's just my background."

He consults the questionnaire. "The Imaginary Theater Company?"

Nobody gets it. That's why it's such a good name.

—

Step out of the Miyako Employment Agency and into a mouth. The wall in front of me is plastered over with big posters. Each one features a black-and-white smiling mouth. A single black character like a box under each mouth: □. And under that a word: ORO. Is this an ad for toothpaste or cookies?

2

Tea at Mrs. Nakamura's

Mrs. Nakamura, Mrs. Anaka, Mrs. Minato and Mrs. Fleeman make tea. This is how many of them it takes. Actually only Mrs. Nakamura makes the tea, whisking a shaving brush round the inside of a small gray bowl. Mrs. Anaka, Mrs. Minato and Mrs. Fleeman watch, open-mouthed, marveling at her dexterity. With thumb and forefinger Mrs. Nakamura turns the gray bowl thirty degrees counterclockwise *without* losing her grip on the shaving brush. Mrs. Minato smiles and sighs her astonishment. Repeatedly.

Meanwhile my feet, my calves, my knees and thighs, my big Western butt have all gone sound asleep and my head longs to follow. When they said "tea ceremony" I heard "tea" while they clearly meant "ceremony." Numbness creeps upward from my coccyx. I'm not even kneeling like them. I tried that for about six seconds until cramp set in and it took three of them to untangle me (Mrs. Nakamura, laying out the tea things, pretended not to notice). Then Mrs. Anaka showed me how to half-kneel, half-recline, getting my feet out from under the weight of my monstrous glutes. Not that she said that. Mainly there was a lot of giggling behind hands. To point your feet at someone, Mrs. Anaka explained, is very lewd.

Finally Mrs. Nakamura is finished with the fucking tea. She slides the bowl over to me, turning it just so. I gulp it down before it occurs to me that maybe the one bowl was meant for all five of us. Well I was thirsty, wasn't I? Got off at the wrong subway stop, got on the wrong bus. Got off the wrong bus and onto the right bus but it was so crowded I couldn't get off until three stops after the right one and then only after dislodging the fingers of a little bald guy that had inadvertently got caught in the crack of my ass. They didn't say either, at the Kyoto branch of the Miyako Employment Agency, that Mrs. Nakamura lived halfway up a mountain and that you had to walk along this narrow stone path that runs beside a big storm sewer to get there. Naturally I fell off the path and snapped the strap on my left sandal.

Not that it mattered. When I hobble into Mrs. Nakamura's entry hall I have to leave my sandals on the flagstones before stepping onto the boardwalk that leads to the living room where the other ladies are waiting. They, I notice, all wear pantyhose while the chipped maroon nail polish on my bare right foot (I didn't have time to do both, OK?) glows like neon.

What a tasteful room. Acres of grass matting, walls the color of lemon tea, a low shelf at one end of the room bearing one simple glazed bowl. Above it hangs one of those scroll things with a big black Japanese character painted on it. Must be the one for "anal." Holy smoke.

—

We're sitting on hard flat cushions. Mrs. Nakamura swishes up more tea because the Giantess from the West swallowed the first batch down. No food in sight. I never have much breakfast but you'd think that for a noontime English lesson a woman as rich as Mrs. Nakamura—pearls the size of bicuspids ring her neck—would provide sandwiches or chips-and-dip or something.

After the others have had their thimblefuls of frothy tea Mrs. Nakamura gets up and slides back a couple of big panels. The garden's a wide rectangle layered with arcing rows of stones. Moss covers the stones, a different shade of moss for each stone. The sun strikes the moss, which glitters like a wet sponge except it hasn't rained today. There is a pond about the size of a bath mat, but nothing so vulgar as flowers, just every possible shade of green, like in those paint-by-number sets where you're doing a leafy tree and have to open all the little plastic pots from 19 through 41. The only thing to disturb this fanatically ordered peace is the sound of someone hammering nearby, although "hammering" doesn't get it—more like knocking, discrete taps with minute-long silences between.

We all sit on the boardwalk that runs along two sides of the garden, listening to Mrs. Minato's stomach growl. They all smile at me. I grin back. The lesson begins.

Anyone can teach English. If you've spoken it all your life there's no reason you can't show someone else how.

That's why I had no qualms about telling Mr. Okuda at the agency about the year I spent at the Ontario International School of Languages. So I occasionally balled a guy who went there—his name will come back to me in a moment. Thickest dick I've ever seen. Nearly. Anyway, we crawled through enough pubs together for me to pick up the jargon and the attitude. *Ezra*, with a Georgia accent that came and went depending on whether he was teaching or fucking.

I take out my wallet, lay out three 1,000-yen notes on the boards in front of us.

Mrs. Minato and Mrs. Fleeman lean forward expectantly. Mrs. Nakamura's too cool to evince any real interest. Mrs. Anaka looks a little dozy.

"This is an exercise to give me a sense of your comprehension."

Everyone nods to show they follow so far.

"A man has three mistresses."

An inrush of air from Mrs. Nakamura.

I pick up the note on the left. "The first one he gives $1,000 and tells her she can do whatever she wants with it."

"Anything?" Mrs. Fleeman's eyes gleam.

"Anything."

Mrs. Minato says something in Japanese to Mrs. Fleeman and they have a good giggle behind their hands until Mrs. Nakamura shoots them a look.

"The first woman takes the money, goes to a department store and buys a beautiful suit and a nice pair of shoes."

Mrs. Anaka sits up straight. "With 1,000 yen?"

"Thousand dollar," Mrs. Fleeman explains.

"Ah."

I pick up the middle bill. "The man gives the second mistress $1,000. She goes to a *depaato*, spends $500 on a new hat. She takes the remaining $500 and invests it, doubling her money."

Mrs. Anaka claps her hands.

I pick up the last bill. "The third mistress takes her money and invests all of it, tripling its value."

Mrs. Minato raises her hand. "I have one question."

"Yes?"

"They have to pay money back?"

I'm lost.

"To man," Mrs. Fleeman interprets.

"No. The money is theirs to do with as they please."

Mrs. Fleeman gives Mrs. Minato an I-told-you-so look.

"My question is," I continue, "which mistress is the American?"

Mrs. Minato purses her lips. Mrs. Nakamura looks serene, as though she knows the answer already.

Mrs. Anaka nods her head. "You say again, please."

"Say what?"

"Everything."

Mrs. Minato groans. Whipping the three bills from my hand Mrs. Nakamura slaps them down on the boardwalk and repeats the whole story in rapidfire Japanese. I feel I should say something about only speaking English but don't want to cross Mrs. Nakamura.

Mrs. Anaka laughs. "I know."

Mrs. Nakamura's smile is imperceptible but superior.

"American mistress," Mrs. Anaka announces, "spend all her money." Her eyes dart to me for confirmation.

I shake my head solemnly.

Mrs. Fleeman thinks she has it. "No, American save her money ... she ... three times ... *triple* money!"

"No. Mrs. Nakamura, you want to have a go?"

Mrs. Nakamura thinks about this awhile and says, "I don't really care for guessing games."

I'm left holding the punchline.

Mrs. Anaka grabs on to my arm and shakes it. "Who is American? Who?"

Fuck it. "The one with the big breasts."

Silence. Someone somewhere pounds in another nail. Mrs. Minato and Mrs. Fleeman look startled, as if they can't believe what they've just heard. They look to Mrs. Nakamura for guidance. Mrs. Anaka admires her fingernails in the bright sunlight. Mrs. Nakamura seems to be thinking it over. Her chin rises into the air, her eyes narrow and she laughs soundlessly through her teeth like a cat sneezing.

A joke like that will work as a real icebreaker almost anyplace in the world.

3

The Bolthole makes sense as an Olde English Pub
only if you know that the guy who owns it hasn't
been home in thirty years. Depending on the light
—there is mercifully little in the Bolthole—Mel
looks like Martha Graham on a bad day or John
Hurt on a good one, monkey face shriveled over
pug skull, spidery arms sprinkled with liver spots.

Maybe because I'm new here Mel begins every conver-
sation with the formula, "The longer I've been in Japan the
more I've come to realize ..." Possible endings so far:

"... the less I know about the Japanese."

"... that I'll never feel at home here."

"... Westerners really do smell like stale cooking fat."

"... acupuncture is the only thing that works with piles."

Mel doesn't do much around the Bolthole. The work
he leaves to his barboys, Slim and Flossy, a pair of native
prancers with sculpted black hair, whom Mel either fucks
or is fucked by. My money's on the latter since the idea of
Mel with a hard-on beggars description, buggers digestion.

Slim's the stingy one, smells like one of those scratch-and-sniff ads in a fashion magazine. Flossy gives good measure, as it were, and seems nearly human late in the evening as the Bolthole fills with expats and potato queens of all sexes. When Flossy and Mel are having a spat odds are you won't see your tab at the end of the night. When Slim's mad, he lungers into your gin.

Mel lights up a Peace, blowing smoke upward. "How's the teaching then?"

I shrug.

"Lotta new pupils?"

I explain that my rich ladies on the mountainside are about it, give or take the odd university student who answers my ad in the *Kansai Kamikaze*, the local English-language giveaway.

"And you can keep going on ...?" His question dissolves into richly fugal coughing.

"I'm surviving."

Which is more than can be said for Mel. Twice he makes to continue, twice he hits a wall of phlegm. "There's someone I want you to meet. She teaches too."

Before I can head him off he's waving over a woman from the table in the inglenook.

"Bonnie"—Mel waves a nicotinic claw—"meet Louise. She's new in town. Teaches English as well."

No time to explain my congenital inability to make friends with people who dress entirely in earth tones, Bonnie has already planted herself on the stool next to mine. She leans in close to give me a wincing smile. "How long have you been here, Louise?"

When I tell her three weeks she's amazed at my fending skills. She hunches her shoulders and winces once more. Maybe it's a tic not a grin. "How'd you find your way here?"

"JAL."

"No, silly, I mean how'd you end up at the Bolthole?"

Followed the first *gaijin* loser I saw. "I was passing by ..."

"You're British aren't you. I just love your accent."

"Canadian actually."

"Canada. Oh, you're so lucky!" She must have noticed the confusion on my face. "Such a nice country."

Jesus wept.

"And you've got the National Film Board—they do all those wonderful documentaries."

I'm about to ask her if she's seen the one about the blind Inuit soapstone carver, *Cold Hands, Warm Heart*, but she's way ahead of me.

"I wish we had something like that in America."

"I wish you did too, Bonnie. Are you interested in film?"

"That's why I'm here. I came over to make a series of documentaries on Japanese crafts."

"Really."

"The first three are finished—lacquerware, fan making, cloth dyeing—but our grant ran out before we got to traditional package tying so we're trying to find alternative funding."

"That's too bad."

"Oh I don't mind. I just love it here, don't you?" She eyes my glass. Is that the protocol—I'm supposed to buy the old hand a drink, not vice versa?

"'Love' isn't the first word that comes to mind." I reach

for the crispy seaweed treats Flossy has placed near my elbow.

"Having a hard time of it?" She leans close, humid-eyed.

"Not especially."

"How's your Japanese?"

"Non-existent."

She reaches into her patchwork carpetbag. "I've got the *meishi* of an excellent language *sensei* here somewhere."

"Speak white, dear."

She pulls a rubber-banded stack of calling cards from her billfold. "The business card of this wonderful Japanese teacher."

I look into her empathetic eyes. "I'm really not interested."

"She makes it so much fun, especially if you're one-on-one. She also teaches calligraphy on the side and one weekend out of every month special students are invited for tea ceremony."

"I don't want to learn Japanese."

Bonnie sits up straight. "You don't?"

"Watch this, Bonnie." I signal to Flossy, point at my glass, smile, then point to Bonnie. "I get along just fine."

Bonnie says something to Flossy in Japanese, he says something shorter back, she rattles on for several minutes using her hands a lot, a certain wheedling tone creeps in. He chops her off with a nod and a guttural syllable that in a Mediterranean country would be followed by expectoration.

My GT's on the counter in ten seconds. Slim, Flossy and Mel confer in a far corner: some difficulty seems to have arisen over Bonnie's drink.

"But how'll you manage if you don't learn Japanese?" Bonnie digs into her reticule once more and produces a pack of those clove cigarettes they make in Nepal.

"Please don't smoke." I put my hand on her plump wrist for emphasis.

"Oh, but these aren't tobacco—"

"If they were tobacco I'd ask you for one. The smell of burning cloves nauseates me."

"Really?"

I down half my GT in one swallow. "When I was growing up in Canada I learned the language: English for Alberta, French when I went to Montreal for university. In Vienna for my year abroad I learned German. So you see, Bonnie, I've mastered the lingo every place I've ever lived, and you know what?"

Bonnie, distracted, tries to signal to Slim, who's decided it's time to refold all the barcloths. "What?"

"I never understood anyone and no one understood the first fucking thing about me. So I decided on the plane coming over that Japan would mark a fresh start."

Bonnie snaps her fingers at Flossy, who snaps right back. Mel notices this—he does notice, occasionally—and slaps Flossy, who flees into the kitchen sobbing. "But you'll pick up the basics if you're here any time at all."

"Not if I can help it."

Bonnie's laughter is high and metallic. "You're a real character, Louise."

Mel slopes up to her with a great steaming mug of something that smells like alfalfa left out in the field too long.

Bonnie tilts her head to one side like somebody's precious forty-year-old little girl. *"Arigato,* Mel."

"What *is* that?" I nudge the mug closer to Bonnie.

She shoves it back under my nose. "This wonderful tea they make here with last year's rice. Smell."

"Thanks, I have."

"Where you staying?"

"At the Precious Kitten Inn up by the Silver Pavilion."

"Ginkakuji? You're so lucky, that's one of my favorite temples. Don't you just adore it? Such austerity."

"Actually, I came to Kyoto for the kitsch. Gardens with raked sand ... let me tell you something."

She perches on the edge of her stool, rice steam wreathing her pink cheeks.

"They do it for the tourists. This is a greed culture not an aesthetic one. They're austere only if it pays."

When she's finished laughing she says, "It's a lovely area around Ginkakuji. Kind of expensive though. You have a room and a bath or just a room?"

"Room and bath, breakfast included at the Tigger & Pooh Coffeeshop next door."

"How much do you pay?"

I name a figure.

Her mouth drops open. "That's way too much, even for that neighborhood."

"There's a mini-bar and color TV too."

"You're just there until you find an apartment?"

"I guess. I'm in no hurry."

"You must be doing well then. How many students do you have?"

"Four."

"You can live on that?"

"I have a little something of my own as well. You've heard of remittance men?"

She shakes her head.

"It's where your family pays you to stay away."

"That's what happened to you?"

I nod.

"But that's so sad. You never go back?"

"Not to Alberta."

"What did you do that upset them so much?"

"I was born."

She takes a long pull on her rice tea. "I never know when you're kidding, Louise."

Something must be done about this woman. When I'm ironic she's dead serious, when I'm serious it cracks her up.

4

A Bath with Mrs. Anaka

In the middle of packing to move to cheaper digs, a timid scratching at my door. Miko from the Precious Kitten reception desk. "Please, you have visitor."

No one's ever come to visit me at the Precious Kitten before. Throw a shirt on over my camisole and bound down the stairs behind Miko. The low-ceilinged lobby with its fitted tartan carpet and Louis XIV *fauteuils* is empty.

"Outside please." Miko ducks behind the reception counter.

A short stocky man stands beside a large Bentley. He bows, hands me a card. Does me a lot of good: it's in Japanese. He reaches out with one white-gloved hand and turns the card over for me. The embossed English script spells out CAMILLE ANAKA, R.N.

He bows. "Please you come for bath."

Remind me to change my deodorant. "I'll run get my backpack."

He steps between me and the Precious Kitten glass doors. They slide noiselessly open. "We go now or late." The doors slide to. He goes around to open the back door of the Bentley. I dash around the other side and slip into the front passenger seat. This does not please Glyptoman. As he slides into the elaborately slipcovered driver's seat (why do I get only a lacy antimacassar?) I try to explain my preference for riding shotgun. This involves acting out portions of Stagecoach, with me taking both the John Wayne and Andy Devine roles. I think I'm getting through when the car glides up in front of a stubby dark glass rectangle just off Imadegawa. Looks like a bank although the windows are too dark to see in and there's no sign apart from a silver disk over the revolving door. At the center of the disk is carved a single Japanese character, the only one I've learned so far: □. You pick this one up pretty quick in the subway, it means "Way Out." Bonnie says it's actually the ideogram for "mouth." I stand doubtful before the revolving door until the driver bows me through.

Not a bank. A long narrow garden—they'll tuck one in anywhere—about twenty times as high as it is wide. The driver leads me along a sandy winding path, across a low stone slab that bridges a pool full of carp. Not anything as easy as gold or white or spotted carp, these fish jostling together in the deep green water are plum-colored. More of them than I can count follow our feet across the bridge. A breeze sets flickering the bamboo leaves high above our heads. Light mist spreads out before us. An archway made of a series of crossed shafts of green bamboo juts out of the mist. The driver stops at the archway entrance and bows me in. I glance back over my shoulder. He raises a valedictory hand. I walk between criss-crossed poles. It's like being in an old movie: you can still see the garden perfectly, only sliced into foot-long frames by the bamboo. At the end of the archway a silver elevator door. I look for a button. There isn't one. The doors open, no buttons inside either. The doors close. I descend.

A long way down. A bell rings and the doors part to reveal a girl with black hair dyed copper-bright—she must be fifteen or sixteen—artfully torn jeans and T-shirt scrawled over with English words (*RICH PEOPLE SUCK MY DICK, AGENBITE OF INWIT*). Safety pins and less easily identifiable metal objects pierce her ears, lips, nose, cheeks, tongue. I long to remind the poor kid it's 1985, punk's over, but maybe that's only in my world.

Her voice is pure California. "Hiya, I'm Suki. Mom'll be out in a moment." She leads me down a dimly lighted corridor with walls of thick green glass. You can see right through to other rooms, more transparent walls. Where the corridor curves to the left, Suki opens a narrow metal door with rounded corners and a high sill, like on a ship. "You go on in and get changed. I'll see what's keeping Mom."

Laid out on a low bench, a cloth rectangle. This I know from every place I've stayed: a *yukata*, or light cotton bathrobe, which I suspect the natives, with their passion for wrapping things up, also sleep in. Men wear them even in hotel corridors on their way to and from the vending-machine room where they buy cigarettes and cans of Sapporo or Pocari Sweat.

Fold ye olde cut-offs, camisole and shirt into a neatish pile and slip on the *yukata*. The door opens again and Mrs. Anaka comes in, followed by Suki. Much bowing all around. Yes, I have already met Suki and yes, indeed, Suki has already met me. How warm and sticky it is this time of year. One longs for rain. In Hertford, Hereford and Hampshire, hurricanes hardly happen. Suki now speaks in a high affected voice, the same soft soprano chatter that comes over the public address system in the subway, in department stores and supermarkets, even on the city bus ("We soon will be making a brief stop at the University of Kyoto").

"We are so happy you could come and join us," Suki warbles, apparently sincere. Mrs. Anaka nods with vigor.

"Good timing on your part," I tell Mrs. Anaka. "I was starting to smell a little ripe."

"Lipe?"

"Ripe," Suki elucidates.

Pantomime sniffing my pits. "Ripe."

"We clean you up," Mrs. Anaka announces with a smile, "inside out."

They usher me into a narrow room with a green marble floor. Water streams down one glass wall.

Suki unties the sash of my *yukata*, Mrs. Anaka spins me out of the robe and hangs it on a silver hook near the door. They shed their own robes. Suki's lean as a boy, Mrs. Anaka has one drooping breast and a diagonal scar where the other one used to be. Opening a small cupboard she removes a decanter of amber oil and two sets of spongy mittens. Suki leads me to a low silver rail set into the floor and shows me how to crouch down on it. Her mother dribbles amber liquid over my neck and shoulders, working it in with her spongy mittens until my torso's covered with fragrant foam. Meanwhile Suki has slipped around behind me and performs similar ministrations on my back and buttocks. I feel like a car in one of those drive-through wash-and-wax places: slip your engine into idle and let her roll.

When they've finished with my legs they help me up and lead me to the waterwall. Water neither too hot or too cold sluices me down. Step into it like parting a curtain, step out I'm in a new space so vast it appears to have no walls apart from the rushing water. Mrs. Anaka and Suki appear beside me, Mrs. Anaka's crescent scar gleaming with moisture. Great golden rocks crouch like lions on the warm sand. Between their flanks, still blue pools.

Suki and Mrs. Anaka take my hands and guide me to the nearest pool. A flat rock is set with a large earthenware pitcher and three lidless wooden boxes, each small enough to fit your palm.

I stare at the steam rising off the water.

"The secret is," Suki whispers, "to slide in all at once."

"You think you die," Mrs. Anaka giggles.

Suki kneels on the rock and slips into the water, sleek otter body causing barely a ripple.

Mrs. Anaka pokes my belly. "You next."

In a moment. Suki smiles up at me, face aglow with perspiration.

"Think cool." Mrs. Anaka gives me a quick push.

Heat strips up my body, so hot my skin doesn't feel it. Inside me a volcano fills with churning lava. Water reaches my neck, I open my mouth to scream. What comes out is

a ghostly musical sigh that peels my lips away from my
deliquescing skull, sets free something I hadn't noticed was
caged.

"You all right?" Suki lays a hand on my trembling
shoulder.

Try to speak but nothing comes out, not even a sigh this
time.

"Please relax," Mrs. Anaka says as she plops into the pool.

What they don't understand is that I am relaxed. My
body is not hot, I *am* heat. There is nothing like it. I'd like to
tell them all this … somehow the effort doesn't seem worth
the candle.

Mrs. Anaka busies herself with the little pale wood
boxes and the earthenware jug. Eventually she holds out
one of the boxes to me. I know I should lift my hand out of
the water and accept the box, at the same time this seems a
terrible effort. The box hovers before my eyes, a tiny cone
of salt on the rim.

"It's OK." Suki's lips are next to my ear. She takes the
little box from her mother and holds it to my lips. The clear
liquid is warm and tastes of nothing. Sake. I slurp it up to
general appreciation.

Suki hands the box back to her mother, who promptly
refills it.

The funny thing about sake is that it doesn't make me
drunk. I can put it away and put it away and my speech
never slurs, my step never falters. *Au contraire* my mind grows
increasingly lucid with each drop I drink until, finally, a
scathing clarity washes the world and I spill to all those
around me, friends and strangers alike, the accumulated

truths of a lifetime. Then I either throw up or take a taxi home, whichever comes first.

So it's just us girls lolling around the lava pool, knocking back boxes as fast as Mrs. Anaka can pour them. I'm still not talking, everyone seems comfortable with this. At one point Mrs. Anaka sings a song from her childhood. She was born on an island in the Inland Sea, wherever that is. The song has about a hundred verses, every single one of them unbearably sad. I don't understand a word, tears cool my face. At another point—unless I'm misremembering—Suki hops out of the pool and lightly leaps from lion to gold lion.

I must have dozed off for a minute or three. A small creature scurrying up my inner thighs jolts me awake. Suki lightly snores, head against my shoulder, a silver trickle of saliva tracing down my breast, so it must be Mrs. Anaka, who sits opposite me, eyes closed, head held high, mute steamy deity. The little creature squirms upward by inches. What sharp claws it has. Just as I open my mouth to speak it seeks refuge in my bush. Isn't that something.

The deity's head sways slowly from side to side, humming songs from the Inland Sea while toes creep inside me, way inside, stirring up the old magma once more. And now I have a terrible case of the hiccups, in a couple of different places.

5

The rainy season. Clever of them to call it that, otherwise we would be at a loss to describe the endless stream of piss that descends from heaven, day after day after day. No lightning, no thunder, no light pitterpat of intermittent showers, no brief lulls or breaks of tepid sunshine, just unremitting gray rain, gray air, gray exhaust fumes lying low over the city's white office towers and the blue-tiled roofs of houses and temples.

New digs not far from the old digs: L'Auberge Strawberry Shortcake. Infinitely cheaper. My room is, as they say, Japanese-style, meaning wall-to-wall tatami mats, no furniture other than a low-slung parson's table, the bed's the thinnest imaginable futon that you're supposed to keep rolled away in the cupboard or the maid gets horribly exercised and shakes her baby blue duster first at me, then at the cupboard doors. A two-burner hot plate sits atop the mini-fridge, which is tucked into the niche next to the bog. I also have an air conditioner that, if fed 100-yen coins, rumbles like a freight train while lowering the room temperature not at all. L'Auberge Strawberry Shortcake has also provided me with two *yukata*, a black-and-white television sprouting rabbit ears, a pair of toilet sandals and a pair of hallway sandals (I don't make the rules here), and four flat orange cushions stuffed with ball bearings. These, I'm beginning to gather, thanks to the maid's ceaseless promptings, are meant to function as furniture when the futon's packed away IN THE GODDAM CLOSET where it belongs.

Now this is all very utilitarian and admirable in its way, the Strawberry Shortcake room-in-a-cup, the only problem being there is no comfortable place to sit or lie other than on the tatami mats, which crackle when you move, smell funny and are slippery, the last two especially when it rains. And when does it not?

Yesterday I finally located, with Bonnie's tireless help, the English bookshop, which is tucked away down one of those nameless lanes that run between the real streets—you only discover them when you've gotten truly lost on your way to a crucial appointment. Going anyplace during the rainy season is a special chore, not because I mind getting wet but because they're as finicky here about rain as they are about dirt and germs. At the entrance to all the department stores and bigger shops, there are special chrome umbrella receptacles—rows and rows of them, like miniature bike racks. You plug your handle into the slot, take the key and head inside where the girl in the Jackie Kennedy suit bows low to thank you for deigning to enter her pathetic ten-story department store. Or, as is often the case, the umbrella racks are full and you think, Got the little buggers now, I can dribble rainwater all over the silk scarves, the Italian leather goods, the cunning potpourri displays. But no, right next to the umbrella racks is a roll of skinny plastic bags, which are slid down over the offending instrument.

So I've got my umbrella in a transparent sheath—it feels unpleasantly squishy—and I'm collecting thousands of yen worth of English-language books. I get up to the cash, which is run by three girls: one who punches up purchases, another who looks over the first girl's shoulder to make sure she's doing it right, a third who stands alert at one side, paper bag at the ready to receive my items. Juggling slippery umbrella bag, books of various sizes and change purse, I manage to drop the books. Lights flash, sirens go off, bells ring. Storewide alert! Storewide alert! Stupid *gaijin* has made big mess. Girls in navy skirts and perfect white blouses scramble from behind the cash, from the storeroom, from perpetual straightening of the books on their long shelves. We are everywhere crouched down on the wet tile floor, picking up paperbacks and mopping them down with sweet little lace-trimmed hankies, all of us crying, "*Sumimasen! Sumimasen!*" which is Jap for, "I'm so sorry you're such a big clumsy cunt."

With much bowing and many smiles and warm wishes, I eventually extract myself from the English bookstore, buy a box of sushi takeout and a two-liter mini-barrel of Sapporo and trudge home in the deadening rain. Going to have a nice read, aren't I?

It is not possible to read sitting upright on a flat cushion full of ball bearings. I pile the cushions next to each other in two stacks of two and attempt to lie with my elbow resting on one stack, my hip on the other, book on the tatami—except the cushions slide all over the foul-smelling slippery mats. Prop two cushions against the wall, sit on two. Soon my butt's halfway across the room, Patricia Highsmith jammed under my chin. In a rage drag the futon out of the cupboard WHERE IT'S FUCKING WELL MEANT TO BE DURING DAYLIGHT HOURS and roll it into a kind of bolster under which I wedge the cushions so as to half-lie on them, half-lean against the futon. The minute I assume this not entirely uncomfortable posture the maid knocks at the door with fresh dishcloths—she *knows* when I'm attempting un-Japanese practices in the privacy of my room—though since I never ever cook, my old dishtowels are just fine. *Arigato*, you little bitch. I throw *This Sweet Sickness* at the door. I'd rather brave a typhoon than spend another minute inside my room at the Strawberry Shortcake.

If I were forty pounds lighter and eight inches shorter, blue eyes tightly shut, frizzy red hair dyed blue-black and straightened, I might be mistaken, at a great distance and in the rain, for a Japanese woman out for a liquid stroll, picturesque paper umbrella (you know what they charge for a Knirps here?) held low over her eyes. A stone staircase, shallow steps soft with moss, zigzags up the mountainside, small wooden shrines or stone lanterns adorn each landing. Pause at one to pop a hundred-yen coin into the open fishing-tackle box, take out a stick of incense, stand it on end beneath the shrine's low eaves and, using the provided blue box of kitchen matches with Mount Fuji painted on top, set it alight. I haven't a spiritual bone in my large-framed body, just always enjoyed setting stuff on fire. The staircase stretches ever upward. A narrow dirt path winds off into undergrowth behind the shrine. Long yellow grass licks at my ankles, wet leaves deposit rainwater on my shirt, rendering it translucent. A bit of roadkill on the path up ahead. Not quite roadkill—still breathing, quivery flanks streaked with blood, little pile of frightshit beneath a mangled tail. It's funny but somehow you don't expect to see rats in Japan. This one's a beauty, silvery black and twitching. I rummage around in the bushes for an appropriate stick, place it across the rat's neck and step on both ends at once. The flanks deflate a final time.

The path winds onward a ways and dead-ends in a narrow clearing. The little temple, set into the mountainside, looks more Hellenic than Japanese. Classical pediment, low flight of stairs, caryatids instead of columns—not maidens but two elongated smiling stone cats. On the altar next to a tarnished brass bowl full of coins someone has left an iridescent blue feather anchored in a clump of raw meat. A heart of some sort, not quite as large as my fist. Fairly fresh too, at least it *looks* warm.

Time to go. Run back along the path, gooseflesh all over. The stone staircase restores me to myself. It strikes me that a bowl of green tea would be just the thing. Is this girl going native or what?

The staircase ends in the forecourt of one of those big temple compounds I always try to avoid because they swarm with uniformed schoolchildren who gently approach to inquire if they might practice their English and then turn nasty when you refuse. (At Moon Passing Bridge last week, a crocodile of them slashed after me for several blocks crying out, "*Gaijin! Gaijin!*")

The place looks deserted. The lady in the booth at the stockade entrance has no time for me, shoves a pale green slip of paper through the wicket.

Shove it back saying, "English, *kudasai.*"

She rummages around under the counter, comes up with a rumpled pamphlet printed in English and Japanese:

Zenrin-ji Temple
Zenrin-ji, the head temple of Jodu shu (Pure Land Buddhism). Seizan Zenrin-ji sect was founded in 855 by Shinsho. It is generally called Eikando, which derives from Eikan (1032–1111), the seventh head priest ...

Right. These places are always named one thing but called another. The pamphlet also includes a helpful map of the vicinity, in Japanese only of course, with a red swastika turned on its side—a Buddhist symbol, Bonnie claims—to mark some especially sacred spot. Off to one side one of those sandpiles raked into a kind of op-art pattern. Before me a cluster of dark wood buildings jut out of the mountainside, all connected by covered walkways. I leave my sandals and umbrella in one of the metal lockers next to the ticket booth and step onto the walkway.

How pleasant to walk on bare wooden boards in my big bare feet. Yet another faux pas, in the most literal sense: feet are meant to be stockinged or wedged into tiny vinyl slippers but I hadn't set out to go temple visiting today and I fall out of the goddam slippers. The boards creak and pop as I stroll along. The huge pines that shelter the compound give off an ancient balsamy smell that blends with the incense drifting by on damp wafts of air.

In the first temple or pavilion or whatever they call it two guys in rich silk robes with black chiffon tea cozies over bald pates celebrate something. One strikes a big teak toad with a mallet while the other makes buzzing noises through his nose like a swarm of flies round a two-holer on a hot Alberta day. Displayed on the wall, the official Zenrin-ji calendar, glossy with calligraphy and cranes in flight, yours for only 2,200 yen.

Back on the boardwalk I'm passed by two small ladies in brocade suits and nylons the color of old bandages. They bow and, flashing gold-rimmed teeth, hurry up the steps that lead to the pagoda. I let them get a good head start and toil up a different set of stairs toward the next pavilion. It has enormous white wood-and-paper screens all the way around, all of them shut tight except the center front ones, which are open just wide enough for me to look in with one eye.

A slice of high gloomy room, an altar flanked by thick wood columns and elaborate gilt chandeliers in the shape of lotus flowers. Set well back behind the altar I can make out some sort of gold statue standing in a niche. I can see it and I can't see it, so frustrating. The golden gleam pulls me in, the white paper doors keep me out.

Haunt the sides of the building awhile. I know none of the other screens have been left open, but think if I keep returning, keep pacing the narrow wooden walkway, one of them will have glided open while my back was turned. Of course I could simply reach out and slide one of the panels back myself, can feel it in the groove even now, but this doesn't seem right. I feel enough the invasive foreigner, my big feet in every little puddle, my big (only by comparison) tits ballooning out before me into every stranger's face, big butt bumping rows of pedestrians into the gutter each time I turn around.

Return to the front of the pavilion and reapply my eye to the crack. This is all I get. All a stupid *gaijin* deserves.

Soft giggles behind me. The two old ladies in brocade suits. With a hand like a lizard one of them reaches up and pushes back one of the screens. Both ladies smile gold-edged smiles and bow. "*Dozo,*" they say. "*Dozo, dozo.*"

Step over the high threshold, pad across tatami. The ladies scurry on before me, loudly chattering away. They stand before the wide altar and clap twice, bow, stand back, heads tilted to one side. The smaller of the two—the one who slid open the screen—holds up one brown hand and makes what in another world would be considered an extremely obscene gesture. Laughter bends them over. They shuffle backwards across the tatami, bowing, bowing, till they are out the door. The golden after-image of their smiles hovers in the humid air.

The gold Buddha stands in his niche, turning as if to go. He looks back over his left shoulder. He smiles too, not that irritating supercilious smile you see on so many Buddhas but kind of seductive, on the verge of coy. His robe's open to the navel, he has the beginnings of a tummy, and breasts—soft, rounded, warm golden valley between them, not especially feminine or masculine, just sexual, like a late-seventies hipster cat pausing at the far end of the bar. The turn of his body says he's on his way out, he's had it, nothing going down here, what a crowd of losers, while the eyes, the smile, the breasts, the glinting navel say, *"Except for you, darlin'."*

I ought to be going too, really should leave this shrouded room inside the rain. Last call and all, don't want to be here when the lights come up, early day tomorrow, stay to do another line I'll never get to sleep ... All we need is the Bee Gees on the soundtrack, "How Deep Is Your Love?"

And then, I don't know how they did it, his lips part, a voice fills the room, passes down my spine like a warm hand: "Stop dawdling, Louise."

In retrospect, it's easy to see how they rigged it. Doesn't take a rocket scientist to figure out I'm English-speaking. Bunch of novice monks sitting around a rainy afternoon, nothing to do but scare the tourists. How they got my name is a harder matter.

I took a taxi back to the Strawberry Shortcake and slept for twenty-seven hours, missing my regular Friday class with Mrs. Nakamura and company.

6

Party Lights

The Silver Pavilion Supermarket on Shinigawa is like supermarkets back home, except for two things. It smells like it contains real food, soy sauce providing the dominant note, but also ginger, cooking fat, vegetables and meats in various stages of decomposition in the back storeroom and the sharp oily odor of closely stacked fish. The other thing, obviously, is that I can't read any of the labels, except in the small gourmet Western section back by the takeout area, where I sometimes buy a box of Harvest Crunch for twenty bucks, take it home to my room and eat it dry in one sitting. The rest of the store is blind man's bluff with eyes open: stroll up and down the aisles and try to light on something edible. The labels, the very reflectiveness of the Cellophane and foil packages, seem brighter than in the West, most likely because I'm not distracted by meaning.

My favorite section's the party treats aisle, which stretches on and on, bag after bag of unnameable goodies. A lot of the packaging here is transparent but it still leaves you guessing, rather like a specimens collection in a horror-movie laboratory—some contents succeed in looking fungal and embryological at once. These we want to avoid. Others feature bright tarty-colored candies and cocktail snacks. My first several ventures here I tried to locate the seaweed crisps they hand round in small ceramic bowls at the Bolthole, which you'd think would be easy enough. First time thought I'd found the identical thing. When I got it home and opened it, tasted exactly like caramel corn. Second try was indescribable, although now and again I still get the taste of it at the back of my throat.

I also like to wander in the luxury fruit section where $100 buys a nice melon. A choice bunch of muscat grapes fresh in from Umbria costs far more, but then both come in attractive Cellophane-fronted carrying cases, which the help will in turn wrap in a variety of tissues, foil, decorative paper and ribbons and then bag, to keep the elements at bay. These, Mrs. Nakamura has explained, are gift fruits not eating fruits—presentation fruits, as one would take a bottle of wine along when invited to someone's place for dinner. Here you tote along a muskmelon bought on the installment plan.

The produce bins contain bewildering choices, many looking decidedly risky, like the petrified purple cauliflower thing or the long earth-colored root with eyes far more plausible than anything found on a potato. Generally I try to stick to the known since I can't go to the unilingual staff, large misshapen legume in one hand, and say, "What in God's name is this?" Which is why I seem to be stalled at the cucumber display, my fingers deep among and around them, thinking of Peter. The aptly named Peter.

Of course he didn't mean to do what he did, who could have? He was crazy, wasn't he, to just go off like that, not a word, a phone number, nothing. Would have to have been crazy to leave me, *nicht wahr?* Don't really think of him very often any more, practically don't think of him at all, except at certain times of the day, each day: on waking, late afternoons, at three in the morning when I inevitably spring to consciousness after an hour of subaqueous sleep. Weird position to be in, missing not the sex but his sex. Fucking wasn't Peter's thing—a cosmic joke in there somewhere, girls—junk kept him not so much flaccid as indifferent. He had one of those dicks that are pretty much the same size up or down. The first time I opened his jeans, in the ladies' room of some reggae hole in Toronto, it came down like a drawbridge—had had it doubled up in there, only way he could wear it without provoking riots.

He was (is?) a Scot, a painter from Glasgow, working in a Queen Street record shop. Not a movie Scot, no charm or thrilling brogue and crinkly haggis-flecked smile, just the cheesy uncut length of him and hair that had gone prematurely gray from the continual stress of scoring. We were the same age when we met, thirty-two, at least that's how old he said he was. Depending on the day he could have been three times—or half—that. The hair that covered his head and pelted his fleshless body created a silver nimbus about him. I oughtn't to have been surprised at how things turned out, he was the most wholly unreliable person I've ever met, that was what I liked about him. He didn't even bother bullshitting. Couldn't betray one's faith because he allowed, encouraged, no faith at all. When you were with him he was there, more or less, in that nodding moment—the best that could be said of him, and the worst. The rest of the world has good intentions and then they invariably fuck up and feel terrible about it and they didn't mean to hurt you, blah-de-blah-blah-blah. The refreshing thing about Peter was that he had no intentions at all beyond his next hit.

Did I say he liked to kiss? I can manage without fucking—most of the guys who do it at all have no idea beyond themselves—*never* without kissing. We'd lie on the mattress in his borrowed and underheated loft and neck away the hours between the rush and the final fade, his tongue in my mouth, my index finger slicking round the inside of his foreskin. I needed no drugs—at least nothing like Peter's daily shopping list—there was euphoria enough in the sour fungy sweat of him. Did I mention he chainsmoked (unfiltered Players), his saliva dark with nicotine? My shirts at the time always had brown stains on them, the circle of his lips over where the nipple lay and tiny brown squirts of dried blood. Everywhere.

There near the end I should have seen what was coming for he did start fucking. I who had become so adept at finger jobs, handjobs, blowjobs, rimjobs on his limp and unprotesting body was wakened two nights running—one night fore, the next aft. It was like being mounted by a wraith with one muscle left functional and there were great bursts of crimson light behind my eyelids as he touched bottom, as it were, again and again and again. Dryfucking it was, if he came more than a half-dozen times the length of our mutual tenure it wasn't in me. He did have what he called internal orgasms that rattled his ribs against my breasts and caused his bony pelvis to buck like an Appaloosa. The second night as he started to ease it out, which always took some time and caution, I took it in my hand to feel him go. He groaned into my hair and dribbled dark saliva all along my nape.

Expect he's dead by now. Hope so. He always liked to share his works, even long after that had become unfashionable. He said sharing was part of the ritual. I would guess it was also part of the intimacy—he never denied that shooting was better than fucking. A girl named Clelia claimed she saw him in Halifax in '83 or maybe '84 but she would say anything just to get at me, little actress/model cunt.

A high-pitched *sumimasen* from behind me. A freckled white hand reaches past to grab a particularly choice stretch of cucumber. Oh God, *Bonnie*. Small world, she's going to say.

"Louise! Small world. Didn't know you shopped here. Don't you find it a little steep?"

Bonnie's in one of her little-girl dresses, a pinafore really, the pink gingham gathered just under her boobs and then billowing out over her tummy until it ends in pink ruffles a few inches above her round pink knees.

She drops the cucumber into her basket where it comes to rest between a thirty-six-ounce plastic bottle of Coke and a pint container of Häagen-Dazs rum and raisin. "Just stopped in for a few things on my way back from the pool."

I won't ask. If you encourage her in the least way, this is a woman who will take over your life, your thoughts, your home, your very identity. She can't help herself.

"I take an aquafitness class at the university pool. You should come along sometime."

"Exercise makes my heart beat fast."

Bonnie grabs a yellow bell pepper, prods it, smells it, puts it back. "But that's the whole point. You're supposed to ..." She looks up at me. "Louise, aren't you ever serious?"

We head toward the checkout lines, Bonnie surveying the items in my basket. "I'm glad to see you eat healthy."

"Thanks, Mom." I stare at her Coke bottle and ice cream. "Wish I could say the same for you."

"Oh, *these?*"—as though seeing them for the first time. "I'm babysitting my neighbor's five-year-old. Little Gakuji has such a sweet tooth."

As she reaches the cash register and loads her purchases onto the conveyor belt Bonnie says something in Japanese to the checkout girl, who at first looks stupefied and then, as it sinks in, appalled. She starts to load Bonnie's stuff into a plastic bag but Bonnie says something else in Japanese and pushes the girl's hand away. Now the girl looks properly angry, round jaw quivering. Bonnie pulls a blue string bag from her tapestry-work carpetbag and drops her purchases into it. The girl takes Bonnie's thousand-yen notes and carefully places her change on the damp conveyor belt.

"Are you doing anything tonight?" Bonnie says as we stand on the sidewalk under the awning, watching the rain stream down.

"Actually, I really should ..." My mind casts about for a likely imperative.

"There's a party tonight on Yoshidiyama Hill. Should be a lot of fun."

"A *gaijin* party?"

"Mainly Japanese. A few Westerners. It's at Mitzi Yamamura's place. I told you about her. The potter?"

An arts and crafts party. "Will there be demonstrations?"

Bonnie looks confused. "Demonstrations?"

"How to throw a pot, weave a rug, fold a kimono sash, perform vivisection on prisoners of war?"

"Why, no, not that I know of."

"Good. I'll be there."

———

A kimonoed young man with a narrow apricot face answers the door and leads me to the dripping garden where Mrs. Nakamura busily deadheads the bonsais.

"Louise," Mrs. Nakamura bows from the center of the garden. "You are first to arrive. We will have tea while awaiting the others."

Must we? "I'm really not very thirsty, Mrs. Nakamura."

She doesn't appear to hear. Coming to the edge of the boardwalk where I'm standing she steps out of her garden slippers and onto the weathered boards, her white toe-socks glowing in the gray light. The garden shimmers with moisture but the silvery boards are dry as bone.

We sit on an arrangement of indigo cushions and a different servant, a boy really, carries in a silver cartwheel laden with tea things. *Real* tea things: flowered china pot, silver strainer and sugar tongs, *rondelles de citron*, pale flowered cups that look more like spun sugar than porcelain.

"Milk or lemon?"

"Lemon, please."

Mrs. Nakamura hands me a cup. It only starts rattling in its saucer when I take it in my hand. "You have very many nervous energies."

"Much. Nervous energy. You think so?"

"This is common in Westerners, I find." Mrs. Nakamura doesn't look directly at me—hardly anyone here does—but rather appears to address the ornamental tree over my left shoulder. "It is odd though ..."

"Yes?"

"You don't smell like a Westerner."

This is what is known as a Japanese compliment. I stifle the impulse to thank her. "What do I smell like, Mrs. Nakamura?"

"Not like a Japanese." She gives a small smile to indicate this would be too much to ask.

"But how do Westerners smell?" I already know the answer to this one. The first week I was here a girl in a shop filled me in as I was buying underwear. All Westerners smell like rancid butter.

Mrs. Nakamura gazes up at the rectangle of gray sky above her garden wall. "They smell from chemicals first."

"Of," I correct.

"They smell of chemicals. This is from their deodorants, I believe. When you get used to chemical smell, underneath comes something else."

"What?"

She shakes her head. "I don't have words. Fear?" She shakes her head again. "No, it is not that." She studies my wrist, my fingers, the teacup trembling in my hand. "When people are in airplane and the driver says, soon we will crash, there is a word for how they behave then—screaming and other unordered activity?"

"Panic."

She tilts her head. "Like picnic?"

I nod.

"Perhaps it is this."

We sit in silence a few minutes.

"And when it rains," Mrs. Nakamura resumes, "Western-ers smell like, like ..."

She can't bring herself to say it.

"Like ..." I say quietly.

"Like wet dogs!" She gives a brief cat-sneezing laugh.

—

Mrs. Fleeman, Mrs. Minato and Mrs. Anaka, RN, have joined us and are busy laying out their *realia* on the bare boards. This is an idea I got from a book I found at the English bookshop called *Headway: Principles and Practice of English Language Teaching*:

> *Realia*—one way of presenting words by bringing the things they represent into the room. The teacher, or perhaps student, holds up an object (or points to it), says the word and then gets everyone to repeat it.

Last lesson I told everyone to bring in an object, a *thing*, that in some way represents who they are.

Mrs. Minato goes first. She has placed in front of her a leather-bound book. The Gothic gilt lettering spells out *Anne of Green Gables*. She places her small hands on the cover and gently caresses it as she speaks. "This is first book I read in English. Anne is beautiful character, so warm and full of pure feeling. Her life hard but beautiful too. Very nice. When I first read I am girl and I read to my daughters and they read to their daughters. When there is problems in my life, very sad, I read again. When I am lost I think, 'How would Anne go?' She is like a tower for boats to me."

"A tower for boats," I repeat, reluctant to interrupt.

"With big light," Mrs. Minato explains.

"A lighthouse. *Anne of Green Gables* is like a lighthouse for you?"

"Yes." A tear runs down Mrs. Minato's plump cheek. "Please look." She opens the book to the ornate title page. We all lean forward. A violet-ink signature slants across the page: *Lucy Maud Montgomery*.

"Where did you get this, Mrs. Minato?"

"My daughter buy me in New York. Pay pretty much."

"You know Lucy Maud Montgomery and *Anne of Green Gables* are from my country?" I say.

"This is why I bring. I think you understand."

"Lucy Maud Montgomery was from P.E.I."

"P.E.I.?" Mrs. Anaka growls.

"Prince Edward Island. It is a province of Canada."

"Island like Japan?" Mrs. Fleeman says.

"In my country Lucy Maud Montgomery is regarded as a great holy woman. Each spring virgins from all over Canada gather at her island tomb to eat new potatoes and pray for fertility and clean milk."

"Someday I will go to P.E.I. and eat new potatoes too," Mrs. Minato says. She's crying rather a lot now. Mrs. Anaka, R.N., beringed hands apparently as talented as her toes, enthusiastically massages Mrs. Minato's shoulders.

"Mrs. Fleeman," I say. "Show us what you brought."

Mrs. Fleeman holds up a copy of *Fortune*, then flips it open to a photograph of a small man in horn-rimmed glasses

and a gray suit who stands before a glittering black sky-
scraper. "This is my husband Tommy. He very good man."

"Very rich man," Mrs. Anaka mutters, digging deep into
Mrs. Minato's shoulders.

"When I meet him I am only poor dancer"—Mrs. Anaka
whispers something into Mrs. Minato's ear—"in Manila. He
make me everything I am."

I point to the building. "This is in Tokyo?"

Mrs. Fleeman shakes her head. "Hong Kong."

"Mr. Tommy is Chinese Filipino," Mrs. Nakamura explains. "He live ... *lives* in Hong Kong."

"But you live in Japan?" I say to Mrs. Fleeman.

"Safe," Mrs. Fleeman beams.

"He comes here to stay?"

Mrs. Fleeman puts a hand over her mouth and giggles.
"Tommy hate Japan."

"So you go there to visit him?"

"Sometime."

All right. "Mrs. Anaka?"

Camille Anaka, RN, lifts the lid of an embroidered silk
box, folds back a silver cloth and removes a narrow lacquer
box. From the box she unfurls a paper fan with an ivory handle. The parchment stretched across the tines features a roto-
gravure picture of an Aryan-looking Jesus, with blond Breck
Girl hair and pale blue eyes. "This is my grandmother fan."

"Your grandmother's fan?"

Mrs. Anaka looks at me, puzzled. "Yes, my grandmother
fan."

"Your grandmother was Christian?"

Mrs. Anaka nods. "She from Nagasaki."

Everyone nods in unison, as if this explains everything.

"I Christian too," Mrs. Anaka adds.

"Oh?" She looks like she expects an award.

"You are Christian too?" Mrs. Anaka is a prying bitch.

"No."

"Jewish?" Mrs. Fleeman says, touching her nose.

"Nothing. I am nothing."

"Nothing?" They all say it at once, eyes wide.

"Nothing. Mrs. Nakamura, what have you brought?" I can see very well what she has brought: a gray elliptical stone.

Mrs. Nakamura looks down at the stone but doesn't touch it. "I find ... I *found* this stone in a stream near where our country house is, in Kyushu. It was like all other stones in stream, only a little different. When it is in stream long enough it will look like all others. This is why I take it out."

"Oh," Mrs. Minato murmurs.

"And you"—Mrs. Anaka abruptly turns to me—"what have you brought?"

I'm about to say, "I'm the teacher, you nosy cow, I don't have to bring anything," when I reach in my backpack and take out my wallet. I show them the pockmarked snapshot I bought at an Edmonton flea market of a youngish woman with pale skin, large gray eyes and a droopy hat. "This is my late mother."

I spend the rest of the lesson telling them about the nice mother I never met.

—

Yoshidiyama Hill is a pretty swank Kyoto neighborhood—not as nice as the eastern hills where Mrs. Nakamura lives, but not the tacky agglomeration of restaurants, shops, public baths and stucco bungalows found around the Strawberry Shortcake Auberge either. The houses Bonnie and I pass on the road that winds up the hillside are mostly low and modern, and there are no shops at all except for a Rawson's (the Japanese 7-Eleven) at the foot of the hill.

Bonnie has got on her party clothes—all of them, from the looks of it, layers and layers of ballooning silk batik. She looks like an unmade bed at the Rangoon Holiday Inn.

"So is this a sit-around-and-talk party or a drugs-and-dance affair or what?" I ask as we toil up another steep flight of stone stairs.

"Not drugs, that's for sure." Bonnie sets her patchwork carpetbag down on the pavement and takes a few deep breaths. She ought to lay off the clove cigarettes. "Japan is very anti-drug."

"Why didn't my travel agent warn me?"

"But you'll absolutely adore Mitzi Yamamura. She's lived in the West, her English is perfect. Her pots have been shown all over—the Victoria and Albert, the Whitney." She picks up her bag and heads along the dark street. In the distance I can see the stacked neon signs of the Gion pleasure quarter. "There's supposed to be a path along here somewhere."

This would be a much easier country to negotiate if they didn't look upon street addresses as a Western affectation. Up ahead I glimpse flames blooming between thick bamboo plantations.

"This must be it," Bonnie announces and we head up a narrow dirt path. Every few yards a big torch sprouts from the ground cover, flame burning straight in the windless night.

The house looms suddenly above us—a large glass box up on thick wooden pilings. Three Japanese boys stand next to a corrugated metal vat. They grin at Bonnie and me. *"Biiru?"*

"You want a beer?" Bonnie says.

"Sure."

She says something in Japanese. Two of the boys turn away, hands over their mouths, shoulders heaving with suppressed glee. The third hands us our beer.

The entry hall's clogged with shoes and sandals. Bonnie shows me how to prop the toes of my sandals up against the wall so they'll be easier to find later and we climb a narrow spiral staircase.

"This is Minnie's house?" I whisper.

"Mitzi," Bonnie says. "I'm not sure if it's hers or she's just staying here. Pretty neat, huh?"

Groovy. Upstairs it's one long room with square-paned windows running along three sides. At one end there's a low dais or stage. Not a *gaijin* party at all, except for Bonnie and me. Everyone here is like Japanese everywhere—on the subway, in department stores, in the crowded shopping streets at lunchtime. Confronted with difference, they simply refuse to acknowledge it. Bonnie and I are in the room but you couldn't tell by looking at the hundred other people here. Or rather you could by focussing on the space near the spiral staircase where everyone is pointedly not looking.

"Maybe this isn't such a good idea," I'm saying in Bonnie's ear when a tiny woman in a dress that looks like a shiny white sail screams from the stage at the end of the room, "Bonnie, you came!"

Now everyone has permission to look. "Mitzi," Bonnie croons, and the crowd splits down the middle so Bonnie and Mitzi can have a good run at each other, followed by hugs and air-kissing. Close behind Mitzi but hanging back to watch with ostentatious detachment is the most beautiful boy I've ever seen. Black hair hangs to his shoulders, his eyes are large and green. He gives me a look over Mitzi's shoulder, touches two fingers to his lips and slowly, thoroughly, licks them.

While Bonnie fills Mitzi in on her latest grant application for the new documentary on decorative hemp tying, the boy sidles over to me. "I'm Lex."

"Louise."

"American, Louise?"

"No."

"Good. I lived in New York five years. That was enough Americans for me. You a Brit?"

"Canadian. I was in Toronto before I came here."

"Doing what?" He leans in closer so I can get the full effect of the big cat's eyes.

"Theater."

His eyes hover closer still. "Actress?"

I shake my head. "Director."

"Really?"

"You heard of the Imaginary Theater Company?"

"You're with *them*?" He clicks his beer can against mine. "They're supposed to be pretty wild."

"I was with them. We're, er, on hiatus now."

"Funding dried up?"

"Creative differences." Between me myself and I.

He strokes his chin. "I'm an actor."

No kidding. "That why you were in New York?"

He shakes his hair back off his shoulders. "You know the Wooster Group?"

He's with the Wooster Group? "I saw them in Toronto last year. They did *The Crucible* in blackface on acid. Best thing I've seen in years." My turn to lean into his face. "I don't remember you in that."

Lex bows his head shyly. Glossy curtains of hair almost obscure his cheekbones. "I was never really *with* the Wooster Group. They were too commercial for me. There was a split in the company last winter and I joined up with the splinter group—the Rampant Smegmas? We were just getting something off the ground when I had to come back here because my father was ill."

"Oh." I knock back the rest of my beer. "When are you going back?"

He smiles. "As soon as he dies. I hate it here."

"But you are Japanese?"

"My father is. My mom was from New Zealand."

"Does your dad have long to go?"

"I hope not. I'm broke till he croaks."

My turn to click his can. "Here's wishing for a speedy interment."

He winks at me. "He's a pig."

"Do you think it was something in the water when their generation was growing up?"

He can stare for the longest time without those long

lashes ringing down. "All Japanese men are pigs. It's the way they're brought up. And Japan is pig heaven."

"Not only Japan, Lex."

He shakes his head. "I know."

The boy talks the talk. Let's see if he can walk the walk. I tap his beer can with a fingernail. "Ready for another?"

"Sure."

He follows me across the room where Bonnie and Mitzi are surrounded by a clutch of pretty girls singing "I Got Rhythm" in Japanese.

It's so dark on the spiral stair I have to stop and get my bearings. Lex bumps into me, pelvis hard against my butt. I find I have to stop two more times the rest of the way down.

Outside I say, *"Biiru kudasai,"* to the three boys around the vat.

"You speak Japanese," Lex says into my hair.

"You just heard my full vocabulary." The tallest of the three hands me two beers.

"Make sure you keep it that way," Lex says.

"I intend to."

"You learn Japanese and your status here goes way down."

I hold out his beer. He indicates I should hang on to it and digs into the pockets of his narrow black jeans. "I got something for us."

"Yeah?" Attaboy.

In his palm two golden capsules.

"Nice," I say. "What is it?"

"Indigenous product. It's called Serenity."

"What's it do?"

He grins. "It's kind of hard to describe. Anyway, I don't want to force it on you."

I look down at the pretty gold capsules. "Go ahead, force me."

I stick out my tongue. The three boys around the beer vat watch us carefully.

"Grandmother, what a big tongue you have." Lex places the capsule on the tip of my tongue. I flick it back like a lizard and swallow.

He pops the other capsule in his mouth, chases it down with a swallow of beer. The three boys applaud.

"How long's it take?"

Lex consults his wristwatch. "We should be off in ten or fifteen minutes."

"Where do you want to go?"

He stares up at the violet sky. "It's so beautiful here, you almost forget you're in the middle of the city."

Right. "You have to stay close by?"

He nods.

"Mitzi an old family friend?"

"A boy's got to make a living. Anyhow, I don't think you'd like to come with me back to my father's place."

The three beer-vat boys lean way forward, as though memorizing our every word.

I take Lex's hand and bite down on his little finger. Hard. The bone's closer to the surface than I expected. "If this is going to cause problems for you ..."

He inspects the toothmarks on his finger. "No, it's OK. There's a place we can go." He leads me past the gaping beer boys.

The overgrown woods behind the house on stilts are threaded with dirt pathways and lit by tall torches. We follow a twisting path across a stone bridge and past a hut with one big round window.

"What is this place?" I hadn't meant to whisper but that's how it comes out.

"It used to be a restaurant. Mitzi has the idea she's going to turn it into a kind of arts center—you know, kilns for her, dinner theater for me."

I look back at the house on stilts. "Strange restaurant."

Lex looks back too. "I think it was a temple or shrine before that."

"Fuck, Lex, everything here was a temple or shrine at some time or another."

He heads along the path. "That's probably true."

"So what's the difference?"

"Difference?" he calls back over his shoulder.

"Between a temple and a shrine?"

"I'm not sure there is a difference." We've seen the last of the torches and walk along in darkness.

"But I thought"—I hurry to catch up with him—"that temples were Buddhist, so if you see a statue of Buddha it's a temple, and if you don't but it still feels like a holy place and you smell incense, then it's a Shinto shrine."

"Something like that." His voice barely travels the darkness. "Although you'll find shrines within temples and vice versa. What do you care?"

"Who said I care? Do you think you could slow down a little?" But he has already stopped and turned around. My chin bumps against his forehead. "*Sumimasen,*" I say.

"That's three words of Japanese you know." His teeth shine in the dark, translucent as porcelain. "You better be careful."

"Could I be getting off already?" A strange tingling has begun in my sphincter and is working its way up my spine, vertebra by vertebra, as though someone's climbing a golden ladder up my back.

"Maybe. It affects some people faster than others, especially the first time. I'm pretty used to it now."

We're standing in front of an enormous wooden cylinder. "What's that thing?"

He takes my hand and leads me around to the back of the cylinder where he opens a low door and ducks inside, pulling me after him.

I hear the door shut behind me. The darkness is complete now—no moonlight, no city lights and neon bouncing off low mountain cloud, no glistening leaves, no subtly illuminated textures, only this black circumscribed night.

"What is this, Lex?"

He slips away. "This is a temple for the ritual sacrifice of *gaijin* virgins."

"I have nothing to worry about."

I can hear him unbuckling, unzipping, black denim crumpling down his thighs. Suddenly he's against me, my arms go around him—they could make the journey twice—and there's such a sweetness to his skin, it seems as much a part of the dark as the dark itself. There's also the faint odor of fresh beeswax.

He burrows his head between my breasts and we stand like that, not moving, for the longest time. The golden ladder from my butt to my brain is complete, my head's all aglow now. I think it may split open and spew light like a busted Halloween pumpkin.

He's got my shirt open, tits out, his hair silks everywhere, like cool water through the dark. Gold creeps down my neck, illuminating each wet nipple, emerges like a midnight beacon from my belly button.

"I am light," I lean down and murmur in his ear.

"You are the resurrection and the light," he reassures me.

"Louise," he sighs, "Louise."

I start to laugh. "With cheese between her knees."

That brings him up for air. "What?"

"A rhyme from childhood. Adolescence, to be exact."

"I bet"—his fingers ease open the fly buttons of my jeans—"that your sexual awakening came early."

My secret's out. "You can tell that just by touching me?"

"By the way you suck me in."

I spread my legs a little to give his hands more room. "Meet the human vortex, Lex. I've been such a popular girl all my life, at least in the dark. But I have so much light to give."

"I can feel that, Louise. Liquid light."

"Lap it up, baby."

I haven't done a back bend since grade eight. When I close my eyes I can feel my light come shining, from the west down to the east. An eyelid opens in the middle of my forehead and a cone of light blazes out. I must look like a Hare Krishna calendar.

Laughing steadily now, from low in my belly. He pulls me back upright and I can't stop the laughter any more than the light. It all streams out.

Reach for him and miss, reach again and think I've got the finger I bit, except for the fine wiry hair at the base, small plums dangling in a bouncy pouch.

Laughter stops. He stiffens, everywhere but in my hand. He whispers, "You want to stop?"

I say out loud, "Why would I want to do that?"

"Some girls do."

"What girls?"

"Western girls."

"I can think of no good reason."

He's so still now. "You stopped laughing."

"Had to stop sometime." Now I have stopped I'm glad I did. I could have gone too far with my laughter, not come back, at least not in this life. Anyway, the light's enough. And now that I'm growing used to the feel of him in my hand, so is he, slender stalk and sudden dripping blossom.

Then the long inner slide one hears so much about.

"This is all right?" I can't see a fucking thing but know he's looking through the darkness into the light from my eyes.

"This is fine." I'm discovering I can hold him like the greatest doll a girl could have, lift him with my hands, my cunt, throw him high in the air and catch him before he falls. He is so sharp and cunning all the while, stripping me off, scraping me out, layer after layer. Chips off the barnacles and leaves me at last, smooth and seaworthy, ready to ride the flood.

7

The rainy season's over now. It's easy to tell because the rain's stopped falling. Now it hangs in mid-air and they call it humidity. Each morning I get up, walk the three blocks to Rawson's to buy a quart of orange juice and a Silly Cinnamon Surprise, return to my room and change my shirt, soaked through from these matinal exertions. Every time I leave my room, in fact, my tits and shoulders, the small of my back, my underarms and crotch and the crack of my ass immediately blotch over with sweat. The gentle folk of Kyoto, meanwhile, glide past me on the sidewalk, not a drop of perspiration marring their pre-wrinkled ecru linen suits, so used to swimming in this turgid soup it doesn't touch or stain their impeccable bodies, their unsogged souls.

No lessons on the weekend, so after the maid comes to check that the futon's neatly rolled up in the closet, I drag it out again and spread it across the tatami. Many people are unfamiliar with the morning nap, but I've always found it consoling. Breakfast, read one of the stack of discounted Jim Thompsons I found at the English bookshop, then doze for an hour or so. It shortens the day, always a plus, and creates the illusion of a fresh start, although this morning hauling myself out of this second sleep I can't seem to rub the clouds from my eyes. The gray light, inside and out, looks curdled. A gust of sweet cherry scent drifts in the window to remind me that the Auberge is downwind from the heavily deodorized *pissoir* next to the canal, where ancient taxi drivers relieve themselves like racehorses.

Skip lunch, skip dinner, unable to face takeout sushi in my room or myself alone in a restaurant. I find the longer I'm here the less I need to eat. After a certain point hunger, like much else about my former Brobdingnagian life, seems vulgar. Lose another hundred pounds or so, they'll make me an honorary Nip.

By ten p.m. can't stand this tiny room or the smell of moldering tatami a minute longer. *The Killer Inside Me* had me in stitches first time I read it but seems grimmer this time around, the book's inner killer coinciding so neatly with my own.

I walk out into the narrow moonlight. The leaves on the trees along the Shirakawa-dori show a steely sheen. I'll give this place one thing: great town for walking. Doesn't seem to be any crime or even much rape, at least not of Canadian giantesses. Men out alone at night are more startled than anything else by my hulking apparition. In groups they tend to giggle and look away. Last week as I rambled through the entertainment quarter, which at night always has a green cast from neon shining through the willow trees that line the canals, it struck me I was getting more stares than usually allotted an unaccompanied *gaijin* girl in such a touristy part of town. I glanced over my shoulder and four really baked Japanese boys walked in a neat line behind me, carefully and alas—accurately imitating my walk: the hunched shoulders, rolling buttocks and slightly pigeon-toed gait made familiar to me years ago by hordes of teenage tormentors.

Most men in Kyoto are more likely to ignore me altogether, as though I'm an unscalable peak that therefore insults Japanese manhood: ignore it, like the rape of Nanking and Korean comfort women, and it will go away. I'm only guessing this is the case, knowing next to nothing about Japanese men. Obviously it's misleading to generalize from Lex. (I have yet to hear from him but remain unsurprised—assuming messages for me at the Strawberry Shortcake ever make it past the maid—since Mitzi is his meal ticket after all.)

But if he doesn't count as a true Japanese male, what does? There are the scowlers in the subways and rubber-booted fishmongers who, with their early morning hawking, leave trails of gleaming half-opened oysters along the cement floor. The tooth-sucking taxi drivers given to silent tantrums over too much luggage or unclear directions. Middle management types here look much like middle management types anywhere, and who gives a fuck what makes them tick? Eel-hipped nineteen-year-olds with hair curved artfully over one eye travel the night in packs of twelve and smell of Ralph Lauren's Polo, Big Macs and dried vomit. The point is, it's hard to figure out what's male here, what's valued as masculine. Maybe it's just like at home, where everything is as long as it's got a dick.

Went to a movie the other night, a real Japanese one with no English subtitles, just for the hell of it. I was pulled in by the poster, which featured a smiling dog beside a stretch of railroad track. Have I mentioned that I love dogs? And movies about them? So I'm sitting in the darkened theater, it's the seven o'clock feature and instead of the expected roomful of squalling brats I'm surrounded by middle-aged men in suits, all of them chain-smoking. The lights go down, there's some commercials and public service messages—Buy Pocky Chocolate Straws! So Full of Life!, what to do when the Big Quake hits—about twenty minutes of trailers, all of them for movies (or maybe it's just one long fiery movie) about car racing, or rather car crashing.

The lights go all the way down, the feature begins. What a cute dog, like a three-quarter-scale husky except with a fluffier ruff. Disconcerting sky blue eyes. For the longest time nothing happens, as in most Japanese movies. Then everyone, including the dog, commits suicide. Just kidding. The dog—if I understood correctly, his name is Hatchko—hangs out with his master, a professor at a big university. From the clothes and cars it looks like the 1920s or '30s. The setting could be Tokyo, but certainly not the Tokyo I visited. I seem to remember reading somewhere that Tokyo was more completely flattened, reduced to bone and ash, than either Hiroshima or Nagasaki, although the A-bomb wasn't used on Tokyo, only firebombing, carpet bombing or whatever they called it then. In the movie pre-war Tokyo looks like a nice place, lots of parks and trees and low yellow brick buildings, trolley cars, small wooden houses, men in elegant European suits with newspapers tucked urbanely under one arm and women in kimonos scurrying along neat laneways.

Each morning little Hatchko accompanies his master, who's getting on in years, to the train station, watches him board and returns to the old guy's bachelor digs alone. Then, as the day fades, some doggy instinct prompts Hatchko to find his way back to the station to greet his returning master in a dignified Japanese dog sort of way. No slurpy kisses or unruly leaps into the air, the plume tail waves discreetly, like the Queen during a royal progress. This back and forth to the station goes on and on and on, interspersed with an underdeveloped subplot about the unhappy love life of the professor's only living relative, a bohemian niece who smokes cigarettes in a long ivory holder, wears Western clothes and hangs with louche company in a dive with patched-over shoji screens.

Abruptly, the professor keels over in the middle of a lecture. Myocardial infarction is my diagnosis. No one thinks to inform the dog, the niece so tangled in a web of self-indulgence that she forgets to attend the old man's funeral or even dispose of his worldly goods and close his small house. Poor Hatchko, slowly dying of hunger, his coat decreasingly sleek, nevertheless goes each evening to the train station and sits, alert, pathetic, by the side of track number seven, and when the train arrives without his master, Hatchko wearily wends his way home to the empty, cobweb-hung cottage.

Time passes, the seasons change inexorably in Fujicolor montages of autumn leaves, blowing snow, tremulous cherry blossoms, full-flowing mountain streams. Hatchko returns to the station, evening after evening, until one gray twilight he collapses on the platform and dies. The station master and the arriving passengers, who have come to look forward to the dog's stoic if slightly bedraggled presence, are grief-stricken. One of them, a journalist for one of the big dailies, ferrets out Hatchko's tragic story, tracks down and publicly humiliates the niece who, at last recognizing her polluted ways, stops smoking, dons a gorgeous kimono and gives Hatchko a proper burial, his fluffy head ringed with chrysan-themums virtually the same smoky color as his fur. In the movie's coda, she has cleaned up, on her hands and knees, the professor's humble cottage and has herself moved in, having first bought a sweet miniature husky pup.

Sometime around the professor's fatal *crise cardiaque* the men around me begin to weep—not silently, as many a date has done sitting beside me in the West, but uncontrollably, to my unaccustomed eye histrionically. Large white hand-kerchiefs are shaken open, loud sobs vibrate row after row of plush seats, noses trumpet, further sobbing ensues. As the movie continues to unreel I have the sense of being borne along on a slow lachrymal river, for I'm crying too—an orgy of tears, cathartic and yet somehow not, it all seems so easy. Now every time I see one of those stunted mushdogs—they're fucking ubiquitous—pattering along the pavement, my eyes fill and I feel ashamed.

When there's no worry about being mugged or raped by some gomer with a boner for a brain it's amazing how a city will sprawl open for you—no place you can't go as you drift like a ghost from quarter to quarter along pristine sidewalks. I merge with the crowds streaming out of Kawaramachi

Station and let them bear me across the bridge that spans the Kamo to the Gion district, where the geishas are purported to hang out, although how you're supposed to distinguish a real geisha from the rice-powdered and kimonoed hostess girls who work every bar and every besuited customer to the max, I'm uncertain. Weekends the genuine geishas come out to sing and play their samisens and kotos and otherwise click their castanets for the tourist trade. I was supposed to go see them last Sunday with Bonnie. Unfortunately I developed, then cultivated, a headache.

The Gion doesn't look that much different from the rest of Kyoto's night town: cramped and tatty, tiny bars stacked vertically like the cubical neon signs that advertise them. These aren't the kinds of bars you can wander into from the street, for few are even at street level. Most are reached by taking a tiny elevator. The one time I popped into one for a pick-me-up—a place with an English name, Scotch and Cookies, so I somehow assumed I'd be welcome—I stopped the place cold. It was a narrow, low-ceilinged room, like a family room in a Toronto suburb, with a six-stool bar and a sectional sofa set into an alcove. Mini-TVs hung everywhere, with a big-screen one over the bar, all of them playing the same porn video of a tied-up squealing Japanese girl tormented by potbellied and tattooed Japanese men. I didn't get to see how the video turned out because a burly man in a tuxedo crossed his arms over his chest and plowed me back into the elevator.

On the wide banks of the Kamo below, bonfires burn, dark smoke mixing with the fog that creeps in off the shallow water. The damp breeze carries the sound of drunken singing up to me. I wander down a narrow lane, as unpeopled as a Kyoto street ever gets. An old woman with a twig broom strokes down the laneway. Behind the curved plate-glass window of a ritzy coffee shop a young woman in a lemony silk dress clutches a collection of menus like a fan. Farther on a white-gloved taxi driver polishes his rear-view mirror with spit and a gold chamois. A row of vitrines runs down toward the river. The stuff on display is superior to the usual tourist tat—not that it's easy to tell a 300-yen soup bowl from a 300,000-yen one. The *way* the goods are arranged here alerts you it's quality stuff. The lacquerware shop for instance. The tall window holds only five bowls of different sizes ranged on pale wood pedestals. The first bowl's shallow, plum-colored; the second, burnt orange; third and fourth are black as oil; the fifth and largest glows soft gold. I come here every week or so, to this same vitrine, just to look, although I'm fucked if I can explain why. Maybe not so much the bowls themselves as the way they're placed calms me. Smooth and sleek, flawless, they all look so *finished* in a way I've never seen before. Nothing left to be done, nothing left out, and in their simplicity, not a whole lot left in either. Surfaces to slide a finger, a hand across. A tongue. Gazing through the glass I think I'd like to take a bite out of the plum bowl. The glossy shell would shatter like the bright candy jacket of a Smartie, wood dense as chocolate underneath. It's such a dislocating sensation, to discover yourself salivating over lacquer. It sits there silently, gives nothing back but peace, lighted from above by discreet pot lights, lit from within by what?

At the foot of the street a small park gives onto the river. The trees that ring it have been in the city too long, leaves bleached thin and nearly white by exhaust fumes and acid rain. A shallow pool at ring center, a small stone house for a smaller stone god, a low stone bench to contemplate his smirks. My dogs are tired, the bench feels cool against my drooping butt. On the opposite bank of the river through neat ranks of willows I can glimpse the neon of the city proper, the crowds surging noiselessly along gridded streets.

A rustle in the bushes to my left and a high squeak. Fur brushes bare ankle. Leap to my feet. *Rats.* A white kitten tumbles across my shoe. Then another and another and, finally, another, this last fitted out with only half a tail. They put on quite a show, pitifully mewling and crawling back and forth across my feet, except for Screwtail, who leans against my ankle and sneezes every few seconds. I lift him up. He could be hollow he weighs so little. Eyes nearly sealed shut with dried mucus. *Ka-choo. Ka-choo.* He shivers in the palm of my hand. Probably distemper, like barn cats back home. Dead by morning. The others look more lively than healthy, curve of their ribs plain beneath scruffy white fur. Screwtail sneezes again, then pees in my palm. The ammonia smell of so few drops is overpowering. I put him down and wipe my hand on a bush. The ceaseless mewling's getting on my nerves. To make matters worse, sharp cawing begins in the branches over my head. I can make out two limbs hung with big crows, must be close to a dozen of them, huddled together like a funeral choir. The cawing grows louder, the mewling too. The hair on my wrists and neck bristles. Stony cold creeps up my spine. Time to go. The cats tumble off my shoes and scamper after me, except for Screwtail, who has been detained by the crows. A flurry of black wings, a faint cry, fur floating in damp air and the big birds fly back up to their branches. Screwtail lies still in a plum lacquer puddle.

Back on the safe side of the river the crowds carry me along toward a life-size white plastic statue of Colonel Sanders with eyes like an Oriental sage. Behind the counter girls in red-striped caps and aprons bid me an exuberant good evening. I reach for one of the red plastic trays but the tallest of the girls dissuades me. She picks up the tray and maneuvers it in front of three girls flashing aluminum tongs. A fifth girl, in heavy black-framed glasses, thrusts a plasticized picture menu into my hand. I point out a Technicolor grouping of leg, breast and wing, set off by a squat brown triangle that may be fried dough and a small styrofoam bowl of bright yellow corn. A sixth girl, squatter than the others, rings up my purchase and hands me my change.

Up a narrow flight of wooden stairs, I sit down at a dollhouse-size table. The other diners affect not to notice that Gullivette has blundered among them. My teeth sink into the crusty chicken, grease runs down my chin. The smell is all wrong, not of fried chicken but rather something antiseptic and sharp like … like ammonia. I tear open the towelette package and try to expunge the cat pee from the palm of my hand. Ineradicable. I devour the rest of the chicken. The bright yellow corn's sweet and tangy. I eat the brown triangle too and still have no idea what it was.

Back down the narrow stairs the tall girl wrests the tray from my hands, brushes waste paper and plastic detritus into the hinged mouth of a wood-veneer trash bin. All six of them shout lusty thanks and good evening as I step back out onto the sidewalk.

The cavity of my mouth is coated in grease, my teeth slide to one side whenever they meet. Touch my forehead—not just damp but wet with sweat. Start running. Crowds freeze in wonder as I career past, hand over mouth, backpack slipping down to the crook of my arm, banging madly against the back of my thigh. Make it as far as the stone steps that lead down to the riverbank, bile charging up my throat. Make the cobbled bank itself. Kids everywhere. Some, flat on their backs, stare up at the violet sky, others crowd around bonfires, singing sad nameless songs. A few solitary figures stagger about. One of these, a boy in a silver windbreaker, belches loudly in my face. The smell of half-digested beer finishes me off. Not quite making the shallow river I vomit onto the shell of a tortoise-shaped stepping stone. Apart from the chicken and my daily Silly Cinnamon Surprise I haven't eaten much. Still, there must have been a vast fermenting stew in the pit of my stomach for when I'm finished and only heave up gulps of fetid air, you can't see the tortoise for my puke.

Stagger back up the gently raked bank. Slip—I don't want to know on what—and down I go. Hear the gravel crunch against my forehead but don't feel a thing. When I raise my head, I can make out a bunch of kids, boys and girls both, crawling toward me across gravel and flattened-down weeds. A boy in a tattered purple sweatshirt pulls a large handkerchief from the back pocket of his jeans and carefully wipes the dirt and sweat from my forehead and nose, the bits of bright corn and fried chicken skin from my lips and chin. Soft hands massage my neck and shoulders. A pony-tailed girl unscrews the cap of a red plaid Thermos bottle and pours hot liquid into my mouth. Miso. I cough and swallow, cough and bring it back up again. A different boy produces another clean handkerchief. Three girls in navy blue school uniforms softly applaud his gallantry. I'm shivering, teeth clack-clack together. One of the uniformed girls begins to sing, the others join in at intervals. A Japanese round. They arrange themselves about my long corpse, bodies layered weightless and warm against me, and we all drift off to sleep by the side of the slow-flowing river.

8

The School of Heartful Purity

Skin eruptions, I find, often follow a night of weird dreams. The only one I remember featured small insects, furry as minks. When provoked (don't ask) they extended to ten or twelve times their usual size and fucked each other silly, the issue of their concupiscence incubators full of enormous Easter eggs. Woke up with not so much a headache as a strange pulsing between and slightly above my eyes. Dream-clammy sheets twisted round my thighs, I tentatively massaged the painful area, expecting to encounter a bump. What it most felt like *before* I touched it was the beginnings of a monster zit. To my fingertips though, my brow felt smooth, nearly concave in that spot. Checking it out in the bathroom mirror I couldn't see a thing, except that maybe the skin looked too smooth and shiny. If it's not an incipient pustule why does it throb so? With my luck it will break the surface and spout magma during my interview.

Lex set it up. Phoned yesterday like it was the most natural thing in the world even if we hadn't spoken since the night he pronged me silly with his skinny dick. Mitzi has a concession to do these big urn things for the courtyard at the School of Heartful Purity on Mount Kurama, and when she heard they were looking for an English dialogue coach, she immediately thought of me. Right. My bet is it was his idea. I'm sure they're one of *those* couples, lots of fucking around but emotionally welded at the hip. She gives him enough leash to boff me in an oversized sake barrel, he provides pornographic pillow talk to stoke the fires of their stale dyad. I don't care if he describes my clit in full bloom if it means I come out the other end with a real job instead of all this freelance shit. Did I say *all*? Mrs. Nakamura and the girls and that koto player in Arasigiyama who phones whenever he has the bread, which is usually never.

Smear my forehead with Noxzema, slip into a demure linen number I nicked at the Holt Renfrew August sales a couple of years ago and take a container of yogurt from the mini-fridge for a quick breakfast. Lid off, it smells like Noxzema too. Nothing keeps in this humidity. Leave it on top of the TV. Maybe the maid will spoon some down and fucking die.

At Demachiyanaga Station fourteen-year-old boys in black military-style tunics and matching caps surge about me along the platform. At first they seem oblivious to my presence, darting around me, mouths open, eyes lowered, hands fidgeting the air. Then the whispered *herro*'s begin, although it's hard to catch any of them moving their lips. As the tram pulls into the station a bunch of them contrive to crowd so close their sweat-smelling bodies lift me off the ground and carry me into the car. They ease me down at the center of a burgundy plush bench. Boys squeeze in on either side, each one pauses to shake my hand. A dozen others hang from the straps above my head so their crotches bob and sway in my face as the car begins its slow ascent, concrete high-rises, a flowered futon flung over every balcony railing, giving way to intricate villages, stretches of rice paddies and the occasional low wooden farmhouse.

A tall boy with long droopy hands and earlobes doffs his cap, plucks from its inner band a blue origami swan and holds it on the runway of his outstretched palm. I lean forward to examine it. Is this an offering and, if so, what is expected in return? The tall boy's bony knee presses into my thigh, although this may be coincidental. He makes a fist, then opens his hand again. The paper swan lies crushed, the boy's fingers splayed about it like the petals of an unpleasant flower. He pops the swan into his mouth, chews thoughtfully, swallows, then licks nearly purple lips. An odd sound comes from low in his throat, almost a purr.

He points to my left breast. "American?"

"Canadian."

He's puzzled.

"Canada," I explain.

He repeats the three syllables. They run up and down the lines of swaying boys until the word has entered their collective vocabulary for all time. A smaller boy stands on tiptoe to whisper in the tall boy's droopy ear.

The tall boy waggles long fingers above his head. "Snow?"

I waggle my fingers. "Snow."

The tram pulls into a rustic station. I crane my neck to read the English sign as it drifts past: ICHIHARA. No town or village, only the long platform lined with bright-colored billboards. Another chorus of *herro's* and the boys flood from the long car, leaving me alone. As the tram pulls away I glimpse them next to the ticket booth. They remove their caps and bow in unison as I ascend.

Kurama's the terminus. I take out the hand-drawn map Lex faxed me and pass through the mountain village, which is mainly souvenir stalls and restaurants full of Japanese tourists. If I get the job I'm going to buy a box of my favorite bean curd candies on my way back.

The road out of town winds through a dense but neatly planted pine forest, sunlight only occasionally striking the needled earth. Up the steep hillside I see orange torii and long flights of stone stairs that lead to small temples. Or shrines. Every few minutes a car passes by, slowing a little so the passengers can gawk at the big *gaijin* who goes mountain climbing in a linen sheath and court shoes.

After a mile or so the valley widens and in the narrow clearing almost at Mount Kurama's peak is the School of Heartful Purity compound, pink stucco buildings fanning out from a slender golden pagoda. A rank of torii, maybe a hundred of them, march up the mountainside, sheltering a stone staircase. I take the stairs two at a time. Trees and scrub flicker past in the gaps between the torii. Halfway up a carillon starts to peal: "Strangers in the Night" as arranged by Busoni.

By the time I reach the top of the stairs and duck out from under the torii tunnel the carillon chimes into an opulent version of "Lara's Theme" from *Dr. Zhivago*. A parking lot, empty but for a few cars and three tourist buses, stretches before me. On the other side of the lot, ornate gold gates. A strip of garden separates them from the parking lot. Topiary trees and shrubs trimmed into chess pieces lead past a flower clock. The big hand's on the purple cabbage and the little one's on a cluster of pink pansies, so it must be nine-fifteen. I'm late.

No one in the thatch-roofed porter's lodge. I try to rattle the gilded gates but they're immovable. Beyond the gates groups of girls in short tartan kilts scurry past, long-sleeved white blouses immaculate in the bright sunlight. They all wear berets—pink, purple, green, blue, a few golds. I want to call out to them but what would I call? *Konnichiwa?* I'd feel silly. Besides, they ignore my presence, even the three girls in green berets who approach the gates carrying a bucket of sudsy water. They kneel down in the fine gravel and scrub the gilded metal with Lucite toothbrushes. Holy smokes, they must be hot in their berets, kilts and thick green knee socks, yet none of them breaks a sweat, while I stand on the wrong side of the golden bars, perspiration shining on my cheeks, a damp Rorschach on the linen between my tits.

I smile at them through the bars and murmur, "*Konnichiwa.*" They don't look up, although one seems on the verge of giggles. "*Sumimasen,*" I whisper. The smirker looks up. I put my palms together, bow my head and say, "Take me to your leader." The girl puts a hand over her mouth and runs across the courtyard. Her companions continue to scrub scrub scrub, scouring gold rosettes and curlicues and carefully patting them dry with soft white cloths.

After a few minutes she returns, bows to me through the bars and says, "*Chotto matte kudasai*," which translates roughly as, "Wait right where you are, foreign bitch." She takes up a cloth and buffs a gilded hinge.

I wander about among the shrubbery chessmen and nearly step on another team of girls—the orange beret brigade—combing the spotless lawn with Lilliputian rakes. "*Sumimasen*," I mumble, "*Sumifuckingmasen*." They don't look up.

At the end of the strip of garden, water sheets down a slab of rose granite. A green granite plinth bears two marble cameos of a couple of Western-looking guys. Underneath the carved Japanese inscription, a plastic tag gives the translation: THE CIRCLE PORTRAITS ARE THE ITALIAN MARBLES OF RICHARD RODGERS AND OSCAR HAMMERSTEIN.

She stands at my side yet I don't know how she got there. Small, pretty, dark hair, dark eyes—in short, exactly like every other girl I've seen through the bars except she's in mufti, a silky silver tunic short enough to reveal neat muscly legs. From the back of the tunic's neck a band of cloth just long enough to catch the breeze flutters like an abbreviated cape. Her running shoes have little silver wings on the heels.

I'm marshaling my nineteen helpful Japanese phrases when in pure Oxbridge tones she says, "Louise Painchaud? I am Hermiko, Mr. Arakawa's personal assistant. He has asked me to apologize for the mix-up at the gate."

Oh sure, I bet he's fucking mortified. Now it's my turn to apologize. "I'm sorry I'm so late. On the map the school looked a lot closer to Kurama Station."

"And I'm afraid the shuttle runs infrequently when there are no performances scheduled," Hermiko says helpfully.

"I didn't know there was a shuttle."

She turns and really looks at me for the first time. This is an odd sensation since making eye contact here is the equivalent of farting in a crowded elevator: it is done, but only if it can't be helped. "You took a taxi all this way?"

"I walked."

Her smile is worldwide. "This is my favorite form of locomotion too."

I look down at her feet. "Next time I'll have more appropriate footwear. Those are great."

"You like them?" She turns one heel so I can get a better look at the embossed silver wings.

"You buy them here?"

"In Tokyo," Hermiko says. "Do you know the Tragic Amusement boutique in Harajuku?"

"I was only in Tokyo a couple of days."

As we pass between a rook and a bishop the great gold gates swing open, the kilted clean-team nowhere in sight.

"If you don't mind," Hermiko says, "we'll pass by Fragrant Orchard Hall. Fire Troupe are in dress rehearsal there. Mr. Arakawa thought you might like to see the girls at work before your interview. Have you seen any of the Heartful Purity international tours?"

I shake my head.

"We have played both Broadway and in London's West

End, but we did not achieve great success in either place. Audiences found us a bit strange."

Imagine that.

Fragrant Orchard Hall and the two buildings that flank it—"Cocoon Small Hall and Joyful Spot Administration Building," Hermiko informs me—look a lot like Lincoln Center, if you can imagine Lincoln Center in pink stucco. Through Fragrant Orchard Hall's glass skin I can make out a high double staircase curved round a pink glass totem pole lighted from within.

"The entire complex," Hermiko explains as plate-glass doors glide open to admit us to the Fragrant Orchard lobby, "was designed by the noted Japanese architect Kon Edo. Do you know his work?"

I shake my head.

"He is one of our great modernist architects. He studied with Corbusier and Niemeyer and ... and ..." She searches for a third name.

"Barbara Cartland?"

Hermiko regards me from under high-arched brows. "I can see that you are very naughty."

Pink-quilted leather doors thud behind us as we enter Fragrant Orchard Auditorium. The wide stage holds a single set, a staircase running from wing to wing, raked sharply back from the footlights. The fifty or so steps end in a high horizon of slow-turning windmills and racing clouds.

Perhaps the idea of Japanese chorus girls has never occurred to you. Until this moment it had never occurred to me. But there they are, scores of them, half dressed as girls, half as boys, all clogging along in brightly varnished wooden shoes, the girls with chrome yellow pigtails poking out below white caps, snappy white pinafores over bright blue skirts, the boys in navy watch caps and matching smocks, all of them, boys and girls, holding large orange cheese balls in their extended hands as they move back and forth along the narrow glass steps singing, in Japanese, a strangely familiar tune.

"What's that song?" I whisper to Hermiko as an amplified voice abruptly jabbers on high. The dancers halt, listen intently and then lift their cheese balls and begin dancing and singing again.

"'The Windmills of Your Mind,'" Hermiko says.

Of course.

The Dutchboys and Dutchgirls swarm to and fro on the high stairs, cheese balls swinging, as an enormous pine armoire descends from the flies on nearly invisible wires. As it descends its walls become transparent. Inside the armoire huddle seven or eight people—two adult couples, two adolescent girls and a tall blond boy—dressed in shabby clothes, a yellow six-pointed star on every sleeve.

"Can you guess what musical this is?" Hermiko asks over the suddenly minor-key sawings of the violins in the pit.

I shake my head.

"The Diary of Anne Frank," Hermiko says.

The younger of the teenage girls moves to the front of the armoire, throws open the doors and belts out the refrain of "The Windmills of Your Mind." The armoire slowly ascends as Anne huddles again with her drably dressed family and friends.

"Some voice that Anne has."

"Isn't she good? But perhaps we ought to hurry along," Hermiko says. "Mr. Arakawa should be ready for us now."

We fairly fly out of the auditorium and enter a series of glass-sided—even the floors are glazed—walkways suspended between the buildings of the Heartful Purity complex. At the top of the Joyful Spot Administration Building Hermiko leads me into a low fan-shaped room, one wall an uninterrupted curve of glass overlooking valley after valley.

From the far end of the room comes a beautiful young woman in a kimono a shade of blue I never expected to see here, the blue you get on an arctic Alberta day when you plunge your shovel into a snowbank and pull out your flashing load: at the bottom of the indentation the shovel leaves, a line of spectral blue. As she approaches—I can hear the rustle of silk while she's still half the room away—the beautiful young woman withers. A cobweb of lines covers her face, as though the silkworms that made her kimono went on working overtime.

She bows low to Hermiko, who does the same, their foreheads almost touching on the way down. Still half bent the beautiful old woman looks up at me. "So tall," she says, straightening in one fluid motion, and laughs behind parchment hands.

"So wrinkled," I'm about to say with complementary politeness when she turns away from Hermiko and me and slides open a set of black lacquer doors. Hermiko slips out of her silver runners. I hop on one leg, then the other, to pry off my court shoes. For once I've managed to wear pantyhose. Through the dark mesh the emerald lacquer on my toenails discreetly shines.

The inner room is so somber it takes my eyes a few moments to adjust. Water whispers somewhere nearby like the beautiful old lady's silk. She leads Hermiko and me along a narrow boardwalk bounded by sunken rectangles filled with elliptical black stones the size and sheen of mussel shells. The boardwalk divides to circle a black basalt basin, filled so full that water constantly slides over the basin's smooth lip. The beautiful old woman hands Hermiko a bamboo-handled dipper. Scooping up a cupful of water Hermiko pours it over her hands. The beautiful old woman pats them dry with a gray cloth. Hermiko hands me the dipper and I bathe my own hands. A bird sings in the gloom, sweet high trills.

The beautiful old lady leads us to a wide expanse of tatami. Silk-covered walls stretch into darkness. I'm about to sit down on one of the flat cushions when Hermiko lightly touches my elbow to indicate I should remain upright. I wish the fucking bird would stop chirping, I'm getting such a head.

Out of the darkness walks the tallest Japanese man I've ever seen, a small gray monkey balanced on one shoulder of his green silk suit. The beautiful old lady bows until her nose nearly touches the tatami. Her lovely lilting voice calls out an appropriate salutation: "We have brought the Western behemoth, sire, for your kind inspection" (my translation). Hermiko bows, not quite so low, and warbles on a bit, nodding in my direction.

Mr. Arakawa looks me up and down, eyes shielded by oval amber lenses in gold frames. The monkey balances on spindly hind legs and looks me up and down too. Mr.

Arakawa gargles a few words low in his throat. Hermiko says, "Mr. Arakawa finds you tall for a woman."

I find his eyes behind amber glass—they're almost level with mine. "Please tell Mr. Arakawa," I say to Hermiko without looking at her, "that he is tall for a Japanese man."

Hermiko steps about six inches away from me, as though to disassociate herself from the words she translates. Mr. Arakawa takes what I said with a fair amount of air sucked in through fine yellow teeth. The monkey looks up at the ceiling and begins to shrill like a demented lark. The skin between and above my eyebrows throbs.

Mr. Arakawa hammers out a couple of paragraphs of boilerplate, which Hermiko renders for me: the School of Heartful Purity's spiritual mission, the necessity of exporting Japan's civilizing culture to an unenlightened world, the recognition that English, however ordinary, unsubtle and egalitarian, nevertheless is this century's lingua franca and the School of Heartful Purity must move with the times ...

My forehead pulses to the rhythm of Hermiko's translation, and what light there is in this windowless preserve seems to brighten and dim with the pulsations. I catch the beautiful old lady glancing at my forehead.

Mr. Arakawa rumbles on and I think I catch the words, "Imaginary Theater Company."

Hermiko says, "Mr. Arakawa would like to hear how you think your experiences as artistic director of Toronto's renowned Imaginary Theater Company may have prepared you for working with the students at the School of Heartful Purity."

My tongue is a wooden shoe, my forehead feels as if it will soon part like the Red Sea and the monkey shrills ever louder. "The Imaginary Theater Company is ..." I begin in a strange thin voice, "as its name suggests, a company dedicated to ..." I am thoroughly stymied. Mr. Arakawa and Hermiko stand awaiting my further reply. The beautiful old lady's eyes are fixed on my throbbing brow.

"Perhaps you could begin by telling us ..." Hermiko improvises.

The monkey gives over singing, reaches skinny arms far out in front of him like a diver about to launch himself over smooth water and sails across the air to land, weightlessly, on my shoulder, where he bounces up and down, eagerly pulling his pud, which, as it lengthens, resembles an albino earthworm.

"Nobu!" the beautiful old lady cries.

The monkey humps my neck, black bean eyes bright with excitement.

"Nobu!" Mr. Arakawa bellows, but nothing's going to distract the little beast from his simian pleasure. He digs his tiny hands deep into my hair and holds on tight as his pelvis judders away just below my ear.

Mr. Arakawa, Hermiko and the beautiful old lady converge on me. Mr. Arakawa unthreads Nobu's pale fingers from my hair while Hermiko strokes my shoulders and the beautiful old lady helpfully cries, "Oh, oh, oh!"

It feels as though something has burst between and above my eyes. Mr. Arakawa, having succeeded in extracting Nobu from my coiffure, stands back aghast, the monkey dangling from one clenched fist. I can feel liquid slowly slither down between my eyes, along the bridge of my nose. Is it pus? Blood? The look in their startled eyes tells me nothing I need to know. Life moves in slow motion now as a drop collects and depends from the tip of my nose. Reflexively my tongue darts out to catch it. It tastes like salt. Like tears.

Mr. Arakawa hands Nobu—hard-on bobbing—to the beautiful old lady, who bears him away.

Somehow I am lying flat on my back on the tatami, my head on a flat cushion. Mr. Arakawa mops my brow with a big silk handkerchief. He barks something at Hermiko, who kneels by my side.

"I will go now for the nurse," she murmurs and flies from the room.

"This," Mr. Arakawa assures me, tear-stained handkerchief covering my forehead, "has never happened before."

9

Dr. Ho darts into the waiting room. A purple scarf flows from the collar of his aubergine velvet smoking jacket.

"Young lady," he says and scurries away.

I am slow to respond, to him, to the world, today. Have I ever been young, or a lady? The Japanese woman in the next chair with a round face like a shining chestnut seems to think he meant me. She pokes my ribs with a sharp finger.

Drift past the dreadlocked receptionist and into the consulting room, expecting to find, you know, a proper doctor's office—small white cubicles, privacy, hushed disclosures and by-rote responses, pale rubber gloves. What I get is a Bach partita played so loud the speakers pop and bibelots rattle on the mantelpiece, a wide room quartered by billowing white drapes. Through the gauzy cloth to my left an old woman slumps in a chair, book open in her lap, stockinged feet up on a wooden footrest. A mountainous belly rises and falls to the rhythm of mechanical snores behind the curtain to my right.

Dr. Ho has disappeared beyond the wafting veils. I study the Benin tribal masks that dot the walls, the big hand-tinted photo of Rita Hayworth in the heavy gold frame over the fireplace. She wears long black gloves and the gravity-defying dress from *Gilda*. The hand tinting makes her skin look like old ivory and there's something funny about her eyes—do I detect the odd epicanthic fold?

A toilet flushes at the far end of the room, a door opens and closes. Dr. Ho parts the filmy drapes like mist, zooms up to me, grabs my elbow and squeezes hard.

"Oh, very bad," he says, "very bad," and turns to lead me, with slightly damp hands, through the veils to an examining table upholstered in chartreuse vinyl. He covers the table with a white flannel sheet and sits me down. Delicate hands on my knees, he stares into my eyes. "How long you so sick?"

"I'm not really sick. Just a headache and ... some skin problems. I think it may be a boil."

"Headache is sick," he reminds me. "It symbol of system imbalance and this and that. My father doctor to last dowager empress of China. Oh, she have the head ..." and we're off on an intricate anecdote about the black pearl the dowager empress either coughed up or swallowed at the moment of her death. Dr. Ho wavers in and out of intelligibility depending on how amused or scandalized he is by the events recounted. Amusement brings on the giggles, for scandal he lowers his voice to a whisper. Like a good foreigner I nod and smile to show I'm getting it all, forgetting he's a foreigner here too.

When he appears to be winding down—I'm not sure if it was he or his father who served the last emperor of China in someplace called Manchukuo—I point to my own unimperial brow. "It throbs a lot."

As he focuses on the spot between and above my eyes, his long white hair, which brushes the purple scarf round his neck, dips down over one eye. "Very strange." He palpates my brow. "Like big pimple only no pimple there and this and that."

"Sometimes it secretes stuff," I mention.

"Stuff?"

"Like ... tears."

"Maybe your third eye sad. We stimulate endorphins, you feel better. Maybe not right away." He reaches for a small glass box. "How often you come?"

I am nonplussed.

"How many times you come to appointment?"

"How often you think I should come?"

"Oh," he tosses his hair, "two three times two weeks, then we see how you do." He removes the lid from the glass box. Four slender silver needles rest on a bed of cotton batting. "You pay that many times?"

"I'm flush," I explain. When Mr. Arakawa hired me at the School of Heartful Purity, he called me into his office and handed me a brown paper bag. Inside were stacks and stacks of 10,000-yen notes. Maybe embarrassment pay for little Nobu.

Dr. Ho's turn to look nonplussed. "'Flush' like toilet?"

"I'm rich."

"But you artist?" he asks, swabbing my forehead with alcohol.

"Sort of."

"So you artist even if you rich. It happen sometime." He inserts the first needle. It stings some but no real pain, only the sense of it sinking through layers of skin, fat, muscle. Something flashes inside my skull and I can *see* the slow penetration.

"I've got a job," I say as he sinks the second needle into my forehead.

"School Heartful Purity." He bends and slaps his thighs. "Funny place—girls wear boys and this and that. You like?"

"I like the money."

"You pay me a lot." He crouches down and pushes a needle into my shin.

"What's that for?"

"Stimulate libido. You pay lot now, more you come less you pay."

"Nothing wrong with my libido. If I come long enough, you pay me?"

He likes that, jokes with a big saucy girl. "We both pay," he says gleefully. "When last time you fuck?"

"Not that long ago." I start to add, "this and that," but Japan is teaching me restraint.

"How long?"

"I don't know. Couple of weeks."

"No good. Light go out you no fuck alla time. What happen Rita Hayworth. She grow old, beauty go, this and that, she stop fucking, light go out like candle in typhoon. No good. Fucking number one for artist."

I start to ask how he knows Rita Hayworth stopped fucking, but then a better question occurs to me. "What's number two?"

He doesn't miss a beat. "Shitting number two for artist."

I should have known.

"When last time you shit?"

"This morning."

"Smell good?"

I try to remember. "Pretty pungent."

"What pungent?"

"Uh, rich."

He claps his hands. "Ha! That very good. Rich lady, rich shit. Good future for you, Louise."

He jumps to his feet and starts playing with my hair. I'm ready to belt him one, nothing I hate worse than someone playing with my hair. Except it's purely professional: he embeds the fourth needle in my ear.

He fiddles with a machine that looks like a stereo amp. From a tangle of wires he sorts out four black alligator clips and attaches them to the needles stuck in me. Black wires connect clips to amp. In one hand he holds a black box like the controls for an old-fashioned toy train set. He fiddles with one knob, my ear starts to tingle. Another knob and an insect bites my shin every two seconds. The last two knobs he turns way up and tiny feet dance a tango across my brow, back and forth, back and forth, dip dip turn.

Holding my shoulders he eases me onto my back. "You want goose pillow?"

Shake my head. I want blank ceiling, I want white veils, Rita Hayworth to watch over my dreams as she tangos in black gloves. Another big girl. Or was she? Sure filled the screen. Can see her so clearly now, even with eyes shut, only the veil between her and me and then not even that for her face is on—no, *in*—the veil now, no longer behind it. I would say my mind is clear, clearer than it has ever been, except that's not saying much. Yet it's not my mind exactly, it's my eyes, even if it can't be them because they're closed. Still, I see. Not everyday things. Apart from Rita Hayworth, as if she was ever an everyday thing. What I see is air and light—I *know* that's what everyone sees—but I see how they fold into each other like pleats of iridescent fabric, more as if air and light were transparent but solid, aspic without the quiver. This new realm is entirely still, a sphere enclosing me. O bright orb! I'm inside air and light and warmth. My skin's gone aspic too, complete transparence. It ought to be awful, for there is my breakfast proceeding peristaltically along my intestine, and yet it's not awful since I can see that everything is part of this nacreous, harmonious sphere and furthermore ...

"Ha, Louise"—Dr. Ho stands over me—"you snore loud like Mr. Kaguchi over there."

"I've never snored in my life," I assure him. He bends and brushes hair away from my damp forehead.

"What we have here," he whispers, "this and that?"

"What?" I try to raise my head but all the weight in the world presses down on it.

"I think we"—his jaw drops—"I think we ..." followed

by a string of words from which I pluck out one that sounds like "pull."

That gets my head off the table. "What are you going to pull?"

His cool fingertips soothe my brow. "Not pull, Louise." He wipes his hands on a white towel with a panda-bear border. His fingers leave crimson streaks. He puts his hands together. "Like oyster," he begins, then slowly parts his palms, a bivalve opening. "Pearl, Louise, you have pearl."

He holds a mirror with a pink plastic frame in front of my face. Sure enough, just above my eyebrows, carefully centered, a perfect shining pearl embedded in the flesh, speckled with blood, about the size of a baby tooth.

10

My first class at Heartful Purity and no one shows up. This strikes me as distinctly un-Japanese, but there's the classroom, tucked into a warren of corridors behind Cocoon Hall, and there are the rows of empty desks, the pristine chalkboards. I check the computer printout from head office to make sure I've got the right place, right time. Then I wait some more. Not that I care if anyone shows up. As long as they pay me, right? Last night as I was moving into my bungalow up at the far end of the compound, Hermiko dropped by with another brown paper bag full of 10,000-yen notes. I haven't even begun to work my way through the bagful Mr. Arakawa gave me.

At eight-twenty I wander down to the Cocoon lobby. Empty except for a half-dozen girls in green tartan skirts and berets down on their knees cleaning the pink marble floor. Each girl has a strip of gaffer's tape wrapped, sticky side out, around one hand. They move in a single row back and forth across the gleaming floor, picking up specks of dust and lint. Their line divides to let me pass. I nod to them but no one looks up.

Pull open one of the heavy doors to Cocoon Hall and step inside. A lot smaller than Fragrant Orchard Hall but way more opulent: blue mirrors in rococo frames, swirled columns of blue marble, silver plush upholstery and drapes, blue wallpaper with silver flocking for the loges, blue crystal chandeliers dripping from the ceiling along with a galaxy of twinkling blue fairy lights. The doors thud closed behind me.

At stage center stands a giant cookie jar. As my eyes adjust to the light I can see that it's not a cookie jar but a woman, more or less, a *giant* woman—the world's largest Aunt Jemima. A Japanese girl, face blackened, torso heavily padded, head kerchiefed, balances atop a gingham dress twenty feet tall. As she sings the Japanese version of "Happiness Is Just a Thing Called Joe," both dress and girl revolve. When the chorus comes Aunt Jemima lifts her voluminous skirts and a couple of dozen dancers—all in blackface, all dressed as field hands, each with a bale of cotton flung over one shoulder—stream out of her petticoats to perform an Agnes de Mille minstrel show. A bale of cotton catches on a stretch of petticoat rickrack and nearly overturns Aunt Jemima.

A middle-aged woman in Ninja getup storms down the aisle shouting shrill imprecations. The taped orchestral accompaniment cuts out, the field hands freeze, only Aunt Jemima continues to revolve. Ninja Woman gives everyone about five minutes' dressing down, after which the field hands creep dispiritedly offstage. Ninja Woman screeches a final word and invisible wires yank Aunt Jemima out of her giant dress and up into the flies.

"Who you?" Ninja Woman turns her tongue on me.

"I'm ..." I head down the center aisle, friendliness all over my foreign face.

"I know who you are." Ninja Woman strides up the aisle not so much to meet me as to block my way. "I am Madame Watanabe, director of Dirt Troupe."

"Dirt Troupe?"

"As all know, four troupes at Heartful Purity School: Air, Water, Fire and Dirt."

I bow in recognition of this fact.

"Dirt best," Madame Watanabe says. "Other directors jealous, that why we here, little theater. Someday we have Fragrant Orchard Hall. This our right."

Banzai, baby. "I like your outfit."

Madame Watanabe looks down at her asymmetrical black pajamas. "Rei Kawakubo."

"I'm sorry, I don't understand Japanese."

"Everyone know Rei Kawakubo. *Comme des Garçons?*"

That Rei Kawakubo.

"What you do in my hall?" She sweeps back the silky sleeves of her pajamas to reveal praying-mantis arms bound in coils of black electrical flex. "You like my bracelets?"

I nod.

"Very expensive. Yohji Yamamoto."

Bet she has an Issey Miyake cork up her ass too. "I'm looking for my students. For English class?"

She readjusts the huge clump of black hair on top of her head. If it's not a wig she should consider changing hairdressers. "Stupid idea. Lose time, only lose time. Girls speak English OK. Always speaking English, I teach English here always. You know Seidenstecker Phonetics?"

"I don't believe I do."

"Best way learn English. Who cares girls know what meaning their songs. Memory, discipline important, drill drill."

"Mr. Arakawa hired me to prepare the students for an all-English production."

She hisses and bows simultaneously, like a balloon de-flating. "Arakawa-*san*, Arakawa-*san*. Your students"—she extends a pajama sleeve toward the blue padded doors—"in lobby."

"The cleaners?"

"I find them," Madame Watanabe says, "sit empty room, lazy lazy. You late, very late. I tell lazy girls, you drill drill till teacher come."

"I was not late."

Madame Watanabe tugs at the black flex constricting her left arm. "Five to eight! I come in room five to eight, no teacher there. Lazy girls sleep in chairs."

"The class doesn't start until eight."

"Good teacher arrive before girls. Set example."

I've always maintained there's no arguing with cunts. "What musical are you rehearsing?"

"*Cabin Innasky.*"

"*Cabin in the Sky?*"

"What I say."

"This is a popular musical in Japan?"

"Will be when Dirt Troupe finish."

"I'd better round up my students."

"Wound up?" Madame Watanabe pushes me up the aisle with her big clump of hair.

I make like a cowboy with a lasso. "To gather into a herd."

"I know," Madame Watanabe says. "Wound up. Like cow."

"Or clock."

That confuses her. I push open the padded doors. The green tartan girls, down on hands and knees, tape up the dirt. Madame Watanabe shrieks at them in Japanese, each piercing phrase ends with a staccato "drill drill."

—

I've got them settled in their desks, they're all lined up, right across the front row. It looks like they've even arranged themselves in order of height, from the small tremulous one over by the windows to the tall butchy girl near the door. They sit straight up, ankles crossed, palms flat on shiny desktops, black eyes focussed on me.

"This isn't going to work."

Maybe they only understand "to work." They reach down to unbuckle matching black leather satchels and pull out bright-colored notebooks and small oblong metal boxes with designs and slogans on the lids. The notebooks they line up rectilinearly in the center of each desk, the metal boxes parallel to the left of each notebook. As one they open the oblong metal boxes and take out pens, pencils and spotless bottles of whiteout.

Jesus fucking wept.

"Come with me, girls." They sit stock-still. I try again. "Everybody stand up."

A panicky rush as they sweep pens, pencils, whiteout, notebooks and metal boxes off their desktops and back into the satchels, which of course must be unbuckled and then rebuckled if the job's to be properly done. They stand at attention beside their desks. The butch one checks to make sure her beret's on at the prescribed angle. The tiny girl at the opposite end of the row gnaws furtively at a cuticle until she sees me looking.

"Follow me, troops," I say and head out the door.

Out in the corridor I stop and look back. They remain standing beside their desks. The butch one has tears in her eyes. "Class over?"

I wave an arm to indicate they should fall in behind me and lead them through the maze of corridors to a small smoking lounge behind Cocoon Hall. Long benches line the silver-papered walls, big blue velvet cushions cover the benches. I pick up a cushion. "Everybody grab one."

A moment of indecision. They all stand staring not at the cushions but at me. The little nervous one finally says, "Which one we take?"

"Any one, goddammit!" I didn't mean to shout but instead of looking hurt she and the others snap to and start grabbing cushions. Once they have an order they can act.

I lead them back to the classroom, throw my cushion on the parquet floor, start shoving desks out of the way. Butch gets right into it, flings one desk all the way across the room where it takes a chunk of plaster out of the wall. The rest of them stand clutching their cushions.

I sit down on mine. They place theirs in a neat single row facing me. Before they sit there's a quiet scramble to retrieve their satchels. They're busily unbuckling when I hold up my hands to stop them. "No books. No pencils, no pens, no whiteout, no pencil cases. Arrange your cushions in a circle."

As you might imagine, this takes some time, for the circle must be just so. Butch patrols to make sure all the cushions line up in a perfect curve.

Pointing to my tits I speak very slowly. "My name is Louise."

They touch their noses and repeat in unison, "My name is Louise."

This could take a while.

I point to my tits again. "I'm Louise. Now you tell me your name and your age." I point to the fidgety little one.

"Michiko," she says. "Sixteen."

We proceed round the circle.

"Noriko, seventeen."

"Fumiko," says a girl who could very well be Noriko's twin except for the large mole on her chin. "Seventeen."

"Akiko. I am nineteen." She points to her chest and for the first time I notice she's wearing white cotton gloves. "I have studied English for many, many years and yet I still make the most deplorable errors. Even when I ..."

"Very good, Akiko. You can be class monitor." Maybe that will shut her up. She bows her head almost to the floor to show how unworthy she is of such an honor.

Last of all Butch opens her mouth and announces in a fine alto, "My name is Keiko."

But where, pray tell, are Harpo, Chico and Zeppo? "How come your names all sound alike?"

"Alike?" the little one (Michiko?) says and shreds another cuticle.

"The same," I explain.

Keiko says, "'Ko' on end of name mean 'little one.'"

"Only for woman," Michiko adds.

Sorry I asked. "What I thought we'd do today is just get to know one another."

Keiko frowns, her voice goes even lower. "We know each other already. All in Fire Troupe."

Thanks a lot, Butch. "But I don't know you. So why don't we start with each of you telling me something about yourself."

"Anything?" asks the girl (Fumiko?) with the mole. She's going into showbiz with a growth?

"Sure." They look terrified by such latitude. "OK then, tell me three things: the name of your hometown, how long you've been at Heartful Purity and why you're here."

Their hands start to flutter and fidget—they're dying to write all this down.

"Michiko, you want to go first?"

Michiko scrambles to her feet.

"No, it's OK, Michiko, sit back down."

Michiko remains standing. "Sitting no good. Must stand for English, breath very bad sitting down."

The other girls cry out, "Posture, diaphragm, drill drill."

"Sit down, Michiko. Relax, it's only English. Lots of people speak it sitting down." Holy smokes, it's going to be a long semester.

—

The English bookshop's practically empty, apart from the phalanx of girls who run the cash, dust the shelves and just generally get underfoot as I try to see what's new in the mystery section. Not too fucking much, I'm here to tell you. Someone should tell Patricia Highsmith to write faster. Ruth Rendell's OK for a laugh now and then but, despite their reputation, Brits don't do crime and mystery very well— they're always so *surprised* by evil. For Americans it's second nature. I wander over into serious fiction and immediately start yawning. All those covers with tasteful reproductions of third-rate paintings and angry lady writers from Manhattan who've just noticed men are lying sacks of shit. I do get a few snickers out of a collection of phlegminist writers called *Long Time Coming*. Like I'm sure.

And there's Bonnie nudging my elbow. "Is that the only copy?" she says and wrenches the book from my hands. "There was a big piece about it in *The Japan Times* that they reprinted from *The New York Times Book Review*. It sounded so wonderful. I just love the Frida Kahlo cover, don't you?" Then she notices my forehead. The wincing smile fades to a grimace. "Louise, what on earth?"

Everyone at Heartful Purity takes the pearl in stride. No one's been so crude as to mention it. I catch some of the younger girls stealing a glance at it from time to time but even on the tram coming down from Kurama the other passengers managed to look without staring and the herds of milling schoolboys gave me a very wide berth.

I fix Bonnie's eyes with mine so she gets a full frontal view of my brow. "Don't you know about *kamikanitami*, Bonnie?"

She's fixated on the fucking thing. "What?"

"*Kamikanitami*, the ancient Japanese art of piercing. The rough translation is 'needle through shrieking skin,' although I'm told that really doesn't do justice to the Japanese trope, which also suggests the forced penetration of a prepubescent virgin in white ankle socks."

"Really?" She's not listening to a word I say.

"A *sensei* who lives on Mount Kurama did it for me. I think it's rather good, don't you?" At that moment I let the pearl shine a little, so it casts a pinlight beam across Bonnie's confused features. Just as suddenly I shut the shine down.

"What was that?" Bonnie says. *Long Time Coming* drops from her hands but is caught before it hits the lino by a bookshop girl with a feather duster in one hand.

"What was what, Bonnie?"

"How'd you make it light up like that?"

I look straight into her startled rabbity eyes. "I don't know what you're talking about."

She lays a soft pink hand on my wrist. "Why don't we go for tea? I know this wonderful place near the Takashimaya *depaato* where they brew up the leavings of—"

"I'm afraid I really don't have time, I have to be back at school by six. Can I take a rain check?"

Bonnie blankly nods.

"How's the filming?"

"Filming?" she says to my forehead. "Oh yes, the camerawoman's flying in from New Zealand on Thursday and then we're going to Kamakura where there's this wonderful little man who makes these amazing natural dyes from goat placenta ..."

I don't get the rest because the English bookshop is invaded by a horde of Mr. and Mrs. Potatoheads. Enormous gray-skinned creatures with butts wider than the aisle trundle about, barely able to counterbalance their huge bellies. I'm about to dive behind the remainder bin for self-protection when I realize it's only a tour group of Americans looking for the bookshop's Kraft Korner where they sell cherry-bark salad bowls and treen salt and pepper shakers at prices only a Japanese would think to charge and only an American would consider paying.

As a passing big guy in a pale green sweatsuit knocks me against the V–Z shelf, Bonnie takes my arm in hers. "I want to hear more about this piercing *sensei*. Do you know if he does tattoos as well? I think he could be an ideal subject for the fifth installment of my documentary on Japanese crafts and traditions." Her face keeps getting closer and closer to mine. She's trying to look *behind* the pearl. "It's amazing how well he's hidden the wire that holds it in place."

"That's the truly unusual thing, Bonnie—there is no wire. It's embedded in the flesh."

"*Really?* And you think that's, uh, hygienic?"

"Show me one thing in this country that isn't."

"Listen, next time you come to town, let's have dinner and you can tell me all about it."

"I'd love that, Bonnie." I give her the tiniest pulse of light from the pearl for emphasis. "I'll call you."

—

That smell. It's all over me like a second sizzling skin before I'm halfway along the path that leads to Hermiko's digs, which are *outside* the Heartful Purity compound (I'd like to know how she swung that). It's been so long since I smelled that particular odor that I'm parting the tendrils of the willow trees surrounding her bungalow before I realize what it is: steak, grilled steak, marinated in garlic mash and lemon juice. Just the way I like it. How did she know? I'd just assumed she was a vegetarian or at best a fish-only type.

The front screens are open but the house is empty. I can see right through to the far wall where another set of open screens gives me a framed view of the entire valley and suggestions of the valleys beyond—everything strangely depthless and layered, like a series of stage flats. The air itself looks wavery, the light darts and shimmers, maybe because I'm looking through a veil of smoke. She must have the Hibachi set up on the back porch.

I walk around the side of the bungalow, cool willow branches trailing over my bare shoulders. Hermiko crouches on a wide flat rock that juts out over the valley. She holds a large glass lens that concentrates the last rays of the setting sun. Two T-bones writhe on the rock at her feet.

"I think they're nearly done." She carefully places the lens on the rock surface.

"I haven't smelled anything like that since I left Alberta." I hand her the bottle of Aligoté I picked up in town. "Strong enough to make me sick."

She picks up a pair of barbecue tongs fashioned to look like two intertwined snakes and turns the meat over. Dark juice runs off onto the rock.

Saliva makes my voice thick. "You want me to run inside and get some plates?"

Hermiko looks at me blankly for a moment. "We're not going to eat these, Louise. This is just something I do for the cats."

"The cats?"

"The cats that roam the mountain. They originally belonged to the temple, as tenders of the sacred fire"—she nods toward Kurama's peak—"but now they run wild. I like to give them a treat from time to time." She must have noticed my crestfallen look. "Do you actually like steak?"

I nod.

"I'm so sorry. I didn't even think … You see, it's hard for me to even consider steak as food. I do like the smell, but the taste—I find it anticlimactic, don't you?"

"The smell blinds me to everything else, I guess."

She stands up. "I've prepared my speciality for you, Louise." She surprises me by kissing my cheek.

Inside, as light drains from the room and shadows drift in like clouds, the bungalow, almost a twin of my own, feels cool as a cave. Hermiko leaves her wicker sandals by the door and pads barefoot back and forth across the crackling tatami. Her small feet are so fine, toes smooth as beans, the skin stretched across her shins taut and translucent. I watch as she chops carrots, cucumbers, onions, turnips and potatoes into thin slices on the cutting board. On a grill set into the floor she places a pan of oil and heats it until it spits. She covers the slices in pale batter and eases them into the hot oil, leaving each slice only a few seconds before she removes it from the heat and places it to drain on a pale cloth. When a dozen slices are done she arranges them on a plate that looks like gold-tinted glass and hands it to me along with a green ceramic dipping bowl. The plate is some substance lighter and more brittle than glass.

"What kind of plate is this?"

Hermiko's busily tossing turnip slices into the oil. "Tortoiseshell. I collect it, you know."

In a restaurant you'd call what Hermiko's making tempura and wolf it down, let the sweet dipping sauce run down your chin. Hermiko and I sit close to the grill, nibble at our lightly battered mixed veg and savor the contrasting textures, the crackling thinness of the shell and the sudden sweet density of carrot or turnip. When we've finished she unfurls long shrimp in the roiling pan. We dangle them into our mouths like fish hooks encrusted with verdigris.

When the light has gone from the room, and the flat rock beyond the windows is as gray as the sky, the cats come creeping—larger than I expected, longer than house cats and skinnier too, with elongated triangular heads and tails that curl and uncurl as they slink out of the trees and across the clearing toward the steaks. Their short fur glows white in the waning light. What a racket as the first one reaches the meat and, holding it in place with both paws, tears off a piece. It's something like a Siamese's meow, petulant, insistent, unpleasant, only multiplied by twenty or thirty: angry babies crawling toward dinner. You can't see the steaks for twitching tails when the first bird, hectoring like a jay but big as a magpie, swoops down from the blackening sky. Then another and another and another. At first it looks like they're going for the cats' eyes with their beaks but at the last second they pull up and drop bright burning embers from three-pronged claws. The embers hit the cats' heads and spines, meowed complaints rise to shrieks. The cats streak back toward the sheltering pines, fine pale coats smudged with soot. The smell of burning fur fouls the air.

"This is getting serious," Hermiko says as she opens my bottle of wine.

"That happens a lot?" I go to the window and look out over the dark valley. The evening turns full night, the birds have gone, the cats disappeared, although from time to time a muffled screech of pain comes from deep in the forest. Two T-shaped bones stripped to whiteness lie on the flat rock.

"It's gotten a lot worse lately." She shakes her head. "I'll call and complain in the morning."

"Who would you call to complain about something like that?"

She looks at me like I'm dim. "The authorities, of course."

11

—

My mother's wire is nothing if not succinct, but then she's paying by the word, isn't she? "Your father dead 7:03 a.m. Hunting accident. Unnecessary you attend burial as cremation his option."

One down, one to go. Does this mean my monthly stipend will increase? Not that it matters, now I'm rolling in Heartful Purity dough.

12

Oro

Communal breakfasts at Heartful Purity take some getting used to, but faculty are strongly encouraged to take meals with the girls in the dining room of the Here Am I residence hall. On mornings when there's class I straggle in at seven or so—serving stops at seven-thirty sharp (just try getting a tofu cruller or a cup of popcorn tea at 7:32). When I arrive at the long table layered in pink damask, the girls have already been up a couple of hours on cleaning detail. Middle-aged ladies in pink aprons and matching kerchiefs bring out trays set with octagonal *bento* chockful of goodies: multicolored sashimi slices, salt plums or cherries, pickles that crack like cap pistols when you bite down on them, a small *morningsalad* strewn with nicely slimy mushrooms and unidentifiable fish parts, a bowl of rice, maybe a bowl of miso too, a little stir of buckwheat noodles as a special Wednesday treat. A couple of weeks here and I find myself coming down to the dining room on Saturdays and Sundays too, when breakfast's offered until the indecently late hour of eight-thirty, because on weekends they serve my favorite thing in the Eastern world: rice gruel. I know it sounds right out of Dickens—"Please, sir, *no* more"—but it's great, thick and pasty and yet with some grit to it as well. Doused in rice syrup it goes down a treat, and really is all I need to carry me through the rest of the day. At this altitude especially, I find that going without two meals out of the quotidian three sharpens the mind and even the eye. Some afternoons colors are so intense they squirm.

Weekends the girls are allowed to sleep in too—no cleaning duties on Saturdays, only a perfunctory ritual purification of all public passageways and lobbies on Sundays. And until six p.m. on Saturdays, when the first civilians arrive for the evening performances, the girls can hang about the grounds in mufti, although what this amounts to is a *toilette* as elaborate and exacting as their weekday routine, with everyone turned out in wholesome frocks, spit-shined pumps and chemically fragrant pantyhose. Except for Keiko, who favors a khaki jumpsuit cinched at the waist with a pigskin cartridge belt. She's allowed some sartorial latitude, for she's being groomed to become a Fire Troupe TopStar. In a couple of years when she, Michiko, Fumiko and the rest of the gang are ready to face the public in full-scale productions, Keiko will play first male lead. In other words, romantic hero (if this were opera, heldentenor), voice trained down to a suitable pitch, hips dieted to the bone, breasts taped flat, shoulders cunningly broadened by the wardrobe mistress, walk swaggered up by the Masculine Comportment instructor—a dainty queen from Nagasaki named Toshiro whose one talent is flawless imitation of the gamut of established macho styles, Western and Oriental.

Already Keiko is rained with perks and privileges unknown to the rest of her cohort. She's expected to be expansive, even loud. The other teachers spoil, coddle and dote on her. The serving ladies in the dining room constantly top up her miso or smuggle her extra bean curd delights. Saturday mornings when she strides into the dining room in her jumpsuit even the older girls pause to appreciate her entrance, which is developing the illusion of a testicular swing. As she eats, origami animals appear as if by magic at her trayside. One by one she painstakingly unfolds and reads, blank-faced, these fancifully pleated mash notes.

On my way out of the dining room I take my mother's telegram out of my pocket, unfold it and read it again, just to make sure he's truly gone. Suddenly a cramp bends me double—don't know if it's the telegram or the extra serving of gruel.

I could use any of the Ladies' Lounges in the Here Am I building—marked by an unfurled pink fan on the door— but something urges me up the hill to my bungalow, even though there are panicky, nearly deliquescent moments when I'm not sure I'll make it. Leap onto the veranda, kick off my shoes and dash across the tatami to the bathroom door, where I wedge my toes into toilet slippers, tear down my trousers and hastily crouch over the porcelain trough. I back off the tiled platform.

Well. I've never seen one quite like that before. I knew his death would bring release, but still. Dr. Ho was right: number two *is* number two for artist. I slip out the gate in the compound wall behind my bungalow and race up the path to Hermiko's. She sits on her front steps, taking the sun.

"You've got to see this." I grab her hand and drag her down the path. The door to the bathroom's ajar as I left it, rich loamy odor spread everywhere. I throw the door all the way open. Hermiko peers in.

"Louise!" she cries and looks at me, eyebrows up near her hairline. "Have you got a camera?"

"Just my old Polaroid."

"Get it." She's practically shouting. For a Japanese.

It's in the futon cupboard, high on a shelf behind stacks of books and boxes. I hand the camera to her, she puts on my toilet slippers and steps into the little room. The flash lights up the doorway. She comes out and we watch the perfect copperplate L swim up out of the glossy white rectangle like a velvety eel.

She places the photo on the shelf next to my bed, murmuring to herself, "This is something … this is really something," as though in a trance. At last she turns to me and says, "Do you know what this means?"

I shake my head.

"You are now most fully yourself." She grins. "Such a propitious day. Let's go shopping."

It never occurred to me to walk from Kurama down to Kyoto—it must be miles and miles—but Hermiko knows a secret shortcut. At first we follow a narrow stream that rushes down the mountainside, both of us so elated by my fecal triumph that we fairly float along. The straight-trunked pines segment the sunlight as we glide, feet off the ground, like racehorses caught by the camera in an act of *léger du pied*. Eventually the stream pours into a shallow river. We stroll along the wide banks but it's as if we move in place and the world slides by like a diorama—the clear river currents spread smooth as paint from a brush, men in shirtsleeves walking inquisitive miniature dogs, a soccer-team scrimmage in red clouds of dust, a hunched old woman retrieving bottles from the beaten weeds. This river joins a wider, fuller one and abruptly we're in the heart of Kyoto.

Shoppers throng the covered sidewalks of Kawaramachi-dori. Hermiko takes my hand and threads us through the crowds. A current of air encapsulates us, we move at three times the speed of the middle-aged ladies with their purses and shopping bags, the hordes of teenage girls in pleated skirts and middy blouses. Nothing can touch us.

We duck into a long high-ceilinged shop. The floor is raw concrete glazed with honey-colored resin, the display racks rusted iron girders, the mirrors long sheets of polished tin with dangerous raggedy edges. The salesgirls take forever to reach us from the far end of the shop, tottering along on sandals with black wooden soles a foot thick. Even barefoot locomotion would be difficult for them, their copper lamé sheathes are that tight. Backlit by chromed automobile headlamps and welders' torches flaring in high niches, in their laborious approach they look like gilded Giacomettis.

Once they do arrive there's a fair amount of bowing, fluttering and eyelash-gnashing over Hermiko, obviously a regular here. She gestures toward me and commands them to break out the canvas circus tents to clothe the Canadian colossus. The girls teeter off to storerooms concealed behind stacks of disused steam-heat radiators and return, eons later, with a single garment that trails over their etiolated arms, glistening like an oil slick.

I'm hustled inside a big corrugated metal smokestack that serves as a changing room. Even in the tin mirror I can tell the dress is sensational. Bias-cut, off one shoulder and barely on the other, it looks like a stretch of gray inner tube until I move—then it shimmers. My body, meanwhile, remains untransformed, the same pasty texture as this morning's gruel.

I step out into the showroom and everyone cries, "Ahh!" The girls clop toward me, long Kyoto faces alight with joy. "*Genki-genki*," they seem to chatter, "*genki-genki*."

"What are they saying?" I whisper to Hermiko.

"Looks good on you."

I glance at myself in a long strip of shredded tin. "They're paid to say that."

"Louise, it's the perfect dress for you. Only someone as … as statuesque as you could carry it off."

The Giacometti girls look on expectantly.

I marshal my most meaningful Japanese phrase: "*Ikura desu ka?*"

One of the girls wavers over and holds a calculator of galvanized steel before my eyes: an LED readout with a comet-tail of zeros.

Hermiko smiles and nods on my behalf, the Giacometti girls burst into applause. For that sum they fucking well should.

Back out on the sidewalk I clutch an oversize shopping bag made of yellowed isinglass. As we stroll along Hermiko says, "Hold out your hand." She dribbles a length of silver chain mail into my palm.

"What's that?"

"A necklace, silly. That's the kind of dress you have to complete."

"But where'd you get it?"

Hermiko grins. "I nicked it while the salesgirls weren't looking."

That Hermiko.

—

We pop round the corner for tea in a narrow multi-level place that's all wrought iron filigree and gold-veined mirrors.

"You want to try the green tea sundae?" Hermiko asks. "It's my favorite."

"Sounds good to me."

The waitress, who wears a tangerine-colored maid's uniform from a *belle époque* farce, bows and scurries away.

Hermiko looks into my eyes. "Happy?"

"Hungry. Shopping always leaves me famished, but then I'm eating for two."

She's startled. "You're not ...?"

I laugh. "I mean I eat enough for two Japanese people. I'm not pregnant and never will be."

Hermiko places her hand on mine. "No?"

"When I had my last abortion I told them to go ahead and take out the whole works."

"You didn't find it"—she pauses, bites her lower lip—"emotionally painful?"

"It was something I'd been thinking about doing for a long time. I always had terrible pain with *mes règles* ..."

"Your what?"

"*Mes règles.* French euphemism for 'period'—what we always said in my family so no one would faint at the thought of vaginal blood. Although 'period' is a euphemism too, isn't it? Anyway, I'd always felt a womb was more trouble than it was worth. So I had them clean it all out."

Hermiko's eyes are full of potential empathy. "It doesn't bother you that you won't be able to have children?"

"Not really."

Her fingers stroke mine. "You could always adopt."

"Even *before* I started menstruating I decided never to have children."

"Really?"

"The one service I can perform for humanity is to become the end of the line as far as my family is concerned."

The French maid arrives with our sundaes, which resemble sundaes only in that they include scoops of ice cream, green tea–flavored, resting on a bed of transparent brown cubes. A thick beady sauce almost covers the cubes—it looks like fish roe only darker. The whole mess is liberally sprinkled with small white marshmallows and Technicolor cherries. With the tiny christening spoon provided I take a few tentative bites.

Hermiko looks on expectantly. "Isn't it something?"

I don't think I've ever tasted unsweetened marshmallows before. They're like fibrous mushroom caps, all texture no taste. The brown cubes are coffee-flavored gelatin and the fish roe turns out to be persimmon pudding, a little runnier than my mother used to make but still with that rich dark dirty taste. The Alberta foothills rear up inside my mouth. It's a flavor I never expected to experience again, especially not mixed with green tea ice cream.

"You like it?" Hermiko prods.

"It's, uh, amazing."

She laughs. "Louise, you're such a good sport. I deliberately ordered the vilest dessert I could think of, just to see how you'd react."

I pick up my spoon. "But I like it. I really do."

"We could go down the street to Baskin-Robbins and order a real sundae."

I try to explain about persimmon pudding, even though it's clear Hermiko's mind has leapt on to a new topic. A bit mercurial, Hermiko.

She stands up. Napkins fly off neighboring tables. "Come on, let's go."

"You want to go back to Kurama already?" It's funny: when I'm there I don't want to leave, it's hard to remember the rest of the world exists. Now we're down in town it seems a shame to head back so soon.

"Not to Kurama," Hermiko says. "We're going to Osaka."

She probably wants to walk. "Isn't that pretty far?"

"It's forty minutes by Shinkansen."

"Oh."

At the train station we head for the ladies' lounge where I change into my new dress and choker and stuff my regular clothes into the isinglass bag. I feel both over- and underdressed for taking the Bullet Train, but when we enter the Green Car (First Class) Hypersaloon we're surrounded by young people of various sexes all dressed for a night on the town. Hermiko removes her short silver cape and ties it around her waist as a kind of flounce. She has the prettiest bare shoulders I've ever seen, lean and muscled. Soon she's chatting up a boy in a snakeskin jacket. The soft rhythm of their Japanese lulls me to sleep.

—

Osaka's more like Tokyo than Kyoto. We ride in a taxi for hours along boulevards too wide and elegant for the clusters of hasty high-rise office towers and boxy buildings stacked with restaurants and boutiques that glide past. Hermiko points out a lighted castle on a hill in the distance and says, "Hideyoshi," but it's gone before I can have a proper look.

We pull up in front of a glass building shaped like an egg resting on its side. Thousands of kids surge back and forth across the wide plaza as men in shirtsleeves and black ties harangue them through bullhorns.

"What is this, Hermiko?"

She darts ahead of me, calling over her shoulder, "Peach-blossom Festival Hall. Stay close to me." She wedges through the chaos with her bare shoulders, her skin has an eerie glow. I look up and a big gold moon bowls out of the clouds.

A phalanx of stocky guys in gray jodhpurs and matching gauntlets block the Peachblossom Festival Hall doors. At Hermiko's approach they step aside, bowing low. Lines of young women in gold uniforms bow us through the lobby and into the theater where our seats are at the exact center, a dozen rows from the stage—the only empty seats left in the cavernous hall. The kids up in the balconies start to chant. It sounds like "Hello, Hello, Hello." As Hermiko and I sit down I hear the rustle of playing cards being shuffled. We turn around: a thousand spectators hold up eight-by-ten glossy cards that together form an enormous black-and-white photo of a smiling mouth. "Hello, Hello, Hello," the balconies echo.

The stage curtain silently divides and retreats, golden smoke billows out of the widening gap and pours over the audience—it tastes like butterscotch. As the smoke clears I can make out a narrow set of stairs sloping up to the flies. A drum roll, a greatly amplified sneeze, the sound of distant rain. Scarlet banners unfurl on either side of the stairs. A golden disk of light appears at the center of each banner, within the disk the image of an enormous golden smiling face, lids smooth as sand dunes, eyebrows like raven feathers.

A mummy undulates at the top of the stairs, swathed in bloodstained bandages. Invisible wires pluck at the bandages, they lift and unspiral, streamers that glisten as if wet when the light catches them.

A slender figure emerges from the shroud, still encased but now by a scaly golden skin. A voice so amplified it seems to rise from the stem of my brain begins to sing. Not much as voices go, what's remarkable is its intimacy—it sings only to me.

The coruscating scaly figure melts into a coil at the top of the stairs and singing still (I don't understand a word, how clear it seems), begins to slither down the black carpeted stairs. From step to step the boneless body pours like a gold Slinky. I feel light-headed, then realize that during this sinuous descent I've forgotten to breathe. It feels like a kind of freedom.

Reaching the stage the figure uncoils into a standing position. The voice at the bottom of my brain leaves off and the scaled costume splits open like a pea pod. A head, a face appears, flesh gold as the scales, but pale, wet, the face on the banners that flank the stairs. A smooth mask. You can't see in. So beautiful, untroubled, there's no need to.

He stands still a moment, torso bare, hair tufted and sweat wet in the spotlight, and I feel such a tug way down where my womb used to be that I can't help myself. I give him a little flash of the pearl, a laser line of pure white light from my brow to his. I can see he gets it, his head starts back. For the first time he smiles the smile of the black-and-white cards the crowd held up. Now everyone chants, "Hello, Hello, Hello."

I shout to Hermiko over the roar, "Why 'Hello'?"

"Not 'Hello,'" she shouts back. "*Oro.* His name."

He shrugs off the rest of the scaly suit, a streak of red paint slashing down his sternum. With thin arms held aloft he urges his worshipers toward calm. Then he wanders over to one side of the staircase—he's down to a gold loincloth that leaves his golden cheeks bare and aglow—where he retrieves an elliptical gold shield shot with streaks of sable and black and spanned by nine strings. He holds the shield against his naked torso so gold skin shines through the shield and runs one hand lightly over the strings. The red paint bleeds in the heat of the lights, trickling down until it stains his loincloth. The whole concert hall seems to sway slightly as he strokes the strings, as though he caresses us too. I'm wet as rain.

Don't know how long he sings, couldn't tell you how many songs. There's no applause, just the sense of thousands breathing together, swaying, drenched. After a while the pearl's wide open, sweeping his face and body like a beacon. I can see his crimsoned torso arch to its touch.

Without warning he puts the shield aside and talks to us in normal conversational tones. This goes on for quite some time.

I nudge Hermiko and whisper, "What's the story?"

"He says he wants the internecine warfare between cat and bird populations to cease immediately. There has been too much pain and bloodshed. The rat population, who have acted as shameless mercenaries throughout the conflict, fighting now for the cats, now the birds, are kindly asked to withdraw to Rodent Island in the Inland Sea, where Oro begs them to cool off awhile and examine their motives."

OK.

Oro comes to the end of his speech. He gives a quick bow and disappears. The curtains close. No applause. The audience seems subdued, even pensive as they file out of Peachblossom Festival Hall.

Hermiko stands, unfastens her cape from around her waist and drapes it over her trembling shoulders. "They always keep this theater far too cool. You want to go backstage?"

—

It smells like backstage anywhere: greasepaint, stale cigarette smoke, Tiger Balm, blind panic. People mill about, it takes some doing to sort them out. The girls in chic linen suits are easy—they're the company types that hover about a star, any star. Publicists, administrative assistants, casual fucks, recently elevated gofers. Each approaches in her turn to sniff about Hermiko. These seriatim encounters have the look of a highly ritualized mating dance. Each girl stands at a forty-five-degree angle to Hermiko, eye contact avoided. Hermiko, with bobbing little bows, explains her mission. Linen-suit girl is hesitant, apologetic, noncommittal. Meeting the great Oro may prove difficult, if not to say impossible, in this century, but if Hermiko and her outlandishly overgrown companion would care to cool their heels ... One linen suit scurries away to be supplanted by another. Hermiko repeats her humble request, the new girl murmurs discouraging formulae. You have to give it to Hermiko: the more she has to repeat herself the more polite, even servile, she becomes.

Meanwhile burly guys in sports jackets stalk about jabbering into walkie-talkies. Off to one side a pocket of teenage girls with the look and smell of the provinces about them: skirts too long, with that hand-sewn droop to them, hair not so much cut as grown. Patiently they wait, swaying slightly, plastic-wrapped bouquets in hand. Clearly the front ranks of the Oro fan club are in for a night of god-gazing. A half-dozen young guys have gathered around a grand piano pushed up against the brick firewall at the back of the stage. One of them chords out "It Never Was You" while another recites the words in a low conversational tone. They can't be much older than the fan club girls, but these guys look like Tokyo to me—money, privilege, sophistication. Identically dressed in baggy gabardine trousers and immaculate oversize white dress shirts with bulbous black cartoon shoes on their small feet, they have eyes only for one another. No wonder. No one else has their distant untouchable beauty and intimidating sleekness, their pampered hair, dipping down over one eye like a comma, or their buffed and lacquered nails, which trail the smoky air.

A wedge of men in long beige trench coats appears stage right and makes straight for Hermiko and me, knocking linen-suited girls and hicks from the sticks flying. The trench coats divide and there stands Oro, in jeans, T-shirt and a navy blazer so perfectly draped it has to be cashmere.

"*Hermiko-san.*" He bows so his torso is parallel to the floor and comes up grinning.

Hermiko bows just as low, comes up for air, bows again, this time in my direction, and says, "My friend, Louise."

He turns to me and tilts back his head to get a good look. Holy smoke, the guy is two feet tall.

Slight exaggeration. If my tits were a shelf—and gravity assures they never will be—Oro could rest his perfect chin on them.

"Hello, Louise." He takes my big paw in both tiny hands. "I am so very pleased to meet you." Like a child looking up at a ridiculously tall tree he doesn't know whether to laugh or climb me.

The widest of the trench coats steps forward and bends down to rumble in Oro's small gold ear.

Oro turns to us. "You will come to supper?"

Hermiko and I nod.

"We will go in the second car." Stage left half a dozen gray trench coats hustle Oro toward a fire exit, except Oro stands right in front of us surrounded by a half-dozen beige trench coats.

Hermiko claps her hands and laughs. "*Kagemusha,*" she cries.

"Hai," Oro says, grinning. *"Kagemusha."* The fire door swings open and the gray trench coats bundle the other Oro into a big silver Daimler idling in the alleyway.

"Shadow warrior," Hermiko explains to me. "Oro's stand-in. An old Japanese tradition."

The widest beige trench coat mutters to Oro.

"We must go as fast as fish," Oro says.

Six beige trench coats, Oro, Hermiko and I thunder down a spiral staircase and along cinderblock corridors lighted at intervals by weak violet bulbs. No one says a word. We reach a freight elevator with doors that recede into floor and ceiling like great steel jaws. It carries us to Level J of a parking garage. A midnight blue Maserati sedan screeches up, the passenger door pops open. Hermiko starts to climb in but one of the trench coats growls at her.

"Wait for the second car," Oro says. "We will go in the second car only."

The door closes and the Maserati pulls away.

An identical sedan appears, tailed by two minivans and a Lincoln. Hermiko and I scramble into the back seat of the second Maserati. Oro rides shotgun.

The white-gloved driver squeals us down the curved ramp and out into the night. Traffic lights apparently mean nothing when you're a big Japanese star. Or maybe Oro and his designated driver just don't give a fuck. Hermiko and I lean this way and that as the driver takes corners on two wheels. Oro and Hermiko babble away in Japanese, every few sentences or so switching to English—not for my benefit though. It's more a natural part of their style, their easy cosmopolitan coolness.

"You played well tonight," Hermiko says as we're shoved together when the driver swerves to avoid a pack of red-jacketed girls who swarm past on gold-painted motor scooters, crimson tail lights glowing.

Oro says something I don't get. They both laugh.

"I was surprised when you started playing my turtle," Hermiko says.

"You know," Oro says, "I searched and searched all over my house—I couldn't find my turtle. Then one morning I woke up and there it was in the corner. I was so happy. 'Welcome back, Turtle,' I said." Perhaps he notices I'm slack-jawed with incomprehension. "Hermiko gave me this turtle when we were only children."

He looks at me as though expecting an intelligent reply. I'm supposed to be elated he's found his fucking turtle?

Hermiko jumps in. "The musical instrument he played tonight? I made it for him."

"Real turtle shell. When Hermiko gave it to me, it had only seven strings. I added two strings for harmony," Oro explains.

"What do you call it?"

Oro looks at me in amazement. "Turtle. I call it Turtle."

Of course.

We pull up at the foot of a high-rise tower that looks grand and jerry-built at once, gleaming like marble swathed in cling wrap. The car noses down a concrete ramp and we're in another parking garage. Oro ushers me and Hermiko into a small elevator and pushes the PH button.

At the top, we step out into a small indoor garden. Across a narrow stone bridge there's a dining room backed by a curving sweep of glass. A kimonoed woman scuttles across the bridge in our direction and, jabbering and bowing, leads us not back across the bridge but along the garden's perimeter. Next to a stone lantern she slides open a grasscloth panel and there at a long lacquer table sit the linen-suit girls, the glossy boys in white shirts, a couple of fan club drones with pilling cardigans spread over their shoulders against the blasting air conditioner and a bunch of middle-aged men in somber business suits. They all applaud as we step out of our shoes and onto the tatami. Another expanse of curved glass gives us an unimpressive view of nighttime Osaka and the illuminated cranes of the harbor beyond.

Oro sits in the place of honor at the center of the table, I'm on his left, Hermiko his right. Endless relays of white-jacketed waiters bring trays of food, which is mainly Japanese although one silver chafing dish contains coq au vin and another a mountain of potato salad. The linen-suit girls make much of my chopstick skills and much more behind their napkins, I suspect, of my gargantuan appetite as they help themselves to a fish gill here, a translucent zucchini slice there. From a ceramic flagon Oro himself makes sure my sake cup's never dry. As the meal continues I'm introduced to everyone except the men in suits at the far end of the table. Each, I notice, wears a small square silver pin on his lapel.

"Who are the *croque-morts?*" I ask Hermiko.

"The what?"

"The undertakers at the end of the table."

"Those are my managers," Oro says.

"So many," Hermiko sighs.

"Not so many." Oro looks offended. "One for television, one for cinema, one for music, one for general accounting and one to watch the other four."

"You're in movies and TV too?" I hat my lashes to convey how deeply he has impressed a simple visitor from the West.

"I have a TV detective series, *Maku Hama: Private Eye*, and many commercials too, *ano* ..."—he counts on tiny fingers —"Kamasutra Hurry-Curry, Skinflints Single Malt Whisky, Georges de la Tour Scented Candles. Also, I make three or four movies a year. I have just finished one. Very weird. You know Jim Jarmusch, the director of *Stranger Than Paradise*?"

I nod.

"My new movie is like that. Would you like to see it?" He pours me another splash of sake.

"Sure."

"You are free tomorrow?"

I glance over his shoulder at Hermiko. "Are we going back to Kurama tonight?"

She shakes her head. "It's too late. We can stay here if you'd like."

"At the restaurant?"

"This is a hotel, Louise."

"OK," I tell Oro, "we'll see your weird movie tomorrow. It's in Japanese?"

He nods. "I'll explain the story for you."

"No problem. I'll have Hermiko there to translate for me."

For an instant he looks straight into my eyes. Can't read his at all—they might as well be obsidian—but something tells me he's pissed off.

When the waiters bring in pots of green tea Oro takes a pack of cigarettes from the inside pocket of his blazer and offers me one.

"What are they?"

He shows me the pale blue label: IMPOSSIBLE CIGARETTES.

With a small jade lighter he fires me up. I catch him— almost—inspecting the pearl.

"You have been in Japan a long time, Louise?"

"No, I ..."

The grasscloth panel slides open and another waiter appears carrying a pagoda of empty plates: a slip of paper flutters between every two. He places the pagoda on the table between Oro and me and bends to whisper in Oro's ear.

"Autographs for the kitchen," Oro explains to me. The waiter hands him a pen and Oro works his way down the plates, signing his name, in English, on each slip of paper.

When he finishes he stands. The business managers, congregated by the curving window, gesture for him to join them. As Hermiko and I pad after him across the tatami it strikes me that the view is different now: the harbor has disappeared and in its place is the illuminated castle Hermiko pointed out to me from the taxi a hundred years ago. A *revolving* restaurant. There's one on top of the TraveLodge back in Lethbridge too. Gave me vertigo. Who says Louise Painchaud hasn't been around?

At the window we stand next to the managers who look straight down. Thirty stories below thousands of Oro fans, all of them looking up.

"Time to go," Oro says. He looks at Hermiko. "You are staying here?"

"It's already taken care of," Hermiko says.

He bows twice and in a Burberry flurry he's gone.

13

The pearl's gone. Kind of a relief, waking up with a smooth brow in a strange hotel. It was nice while it lasted, but too much responsibility.

At ten a man in a beige trench coat rings the doorbell to my room. It plays the opening chords of "Greensleeves" in vibrating electronic tones. I throw on my Heartful Purity respectable teacher's outfit and stuff the iridescent inner-tube dress back into the isinglass bag.

A Bentley idles at curbside. Hermiko waves from the back seat, bottle of Veuve Clicquot in one hand. I slide in next to her.

"Where's Oro?"

She eases the cork out and lets the bottle overflow into two crystal flutes. "He'll join us at the studio."

"It's near here?"

"In Tokyo."

"We're driving all the way to Tokyo to see his bloody film? That'll take hours."

Hermiko wraps my fingers around the flute's slender stem. "And they say the Japanese don't know how to relax. It's Sunday, Louise—you're allowed to play."

The Bentley delivers us to a small airfield south of Osaka. The car drives right out onto the tarmac—something I've only seen done in movies—and deposits us in front of a black helicopter, great silver rotor already throbbing.

The pilot wears a fishing hat studded with fluorescent lures. The collar of his flight suit sports a round enamel pin with Oro's stylized smile embossed on it. He shakes his head when Hermiko offers to fill his silver Thermos cup with champagne.

I must have slept. We hover above a maze of intertwining streets, so narrow I can glimpse only scurrying pedestrians and the occasional bent figure on bike or scooter shooting between the orange or yellow awnings of the shops that line the way. A low brick building with acres of gravel-covered roof swoops under us. Soon we're down in the middle of an empty parking lot enclosed by chain-link so fine it shines like silver lace.

In the utilitarian lobby Hermiko and I trade our shoes for gray paper slippers. A fat girl in a quilted silver jumpsuit leads us along corridor after green-tiled corridor until there he is in the distance standing in front of a door covered in tufted black leather. Alone. I've never seen him alone. Well, onstage in Osaka, but how solitary can you be surrounded by thousands of worshipers? He looks, if anything, smaller—the built-out shoulders of his navy silk suit emphasize the narrowness of his waist, the absence of hips. Minus his entourage he doesn't look, as might be expected, *lost*. On the contrary, he appears even more self-contained, invulnerable even. More complete than anyone I've ever met. Hard not to hate him.

We do the bowing thing, he checks his wristwatch. "Shall we start now? I am so glad you could come." He opens the padded door.

A narrow carpeted room with five rows of plush theater seats, all empty. He starts to usher us into the last row.

"Can we sit down front?" I say. "It doesn't feel like a movie unless I sit in the front row."

"Please." Oro steps aside to let me lead the way.

The lights go down. "I hope you will find it enjoyable," Oro whispers in my ear. Then he turns to whisper to Hermiko. She giggles.

What's not to like? It all takes place in a single white-painted room. No sign of Oro for the first ten minutes. A boy in horn-rimmed glasses taps away at a computer keyboard. A pretty girl in a short shimmery dress brings him tea. They don't say much.

After she leaves Oro emerges from the computer screen, naked, golden skin frosted with rice powder, hair dyed stark white (this must be the Jim Jarmusch connection). Computer boy and Oro hit it off at once, although tea-bringing girl can't seem to see Oro at all. He and computer boy spend long afternoons sipping tea from the same cup. All this is from computer boy's point of view so there are many lingering shots of Oro: Oro reclined in lemony light, Oro against a rough plaster wall lit to replicate the exact color of green tea, Oro supine on the tatami, unthinking eyes focused on the ceiling.

Computer boy spends the rest of the movie moving subtly closer to this rice-powdered apparition. They gradually begin to resemble each other—computer boy discards his glasses, dyes his hair white, on certain hot afternoons takes to going without his shirt. In close-up their profiles move closer and closer together, enormous as approaching planets. Sweat glows on their necks, their skin is flawless—hell, poreless—on the big screen. Just then tea-bringing girl enters the room. Not noticing computer boy and Oro crouched together in a shadowy corner she sits down at the computer and idly taps away. Oro, white hair alight, pours out of the screen. The last ten minutes of the movie are alternating close-ups of Oro and tea-bringing girl in paroxysms of ecstasy, although they never touch, never appear in the same frame. The synthesized musical track runs passionately amok. Computer boy is completely out of the picture.

The lights come up. There's always going to be this problem of proportion, isn't there? I've been watching his face ten feet high and now it's a gold ball the size of a cantaloupe staring up into my eyes. "So, how do you like my film, Louise?"

I glance at Hermiko over his shoulder for some kind of cue. Is this a guy who can take criticism? Hermiko has gone blank on me. But show me a guy who likes, or is even used to, criticism.

"I liked it a lot. I'm not sure how much I understood. The tea girl's there to keep it clean, right?"

"Clean?" Oro rubs his hands together like Lady Macbeth.

"Computer boy clearly has a boner for you."

Short pause as Oro looks at Hermiko, who repeats "boner," followed by a couple of paragraphs of Japanese. Oro's face splits open with laughter. He pounds my shoulder with one small fist. "Louise, you understand! You are so smart."

How hard is it to miss? It's like those Rita Hayworth movies where she's a terrible slut all the way through, right up until the epilogue, when it's revealed that everyone has misconstrued her actions. She was never a terrible slut. Suddenly she's dressed in a demure suit and a cartwheel hat to cover the shiny ensnaring hair and she's out the door with some straight arrow who pops her into his Packard and takes her off to Connecticut where she'll have two flawless children and a soulful Negro maid who becomes her confidant and moral support in times of crisis.

Hermiko wanders off to find the toilet. I stand next to Oro, listening to the sound of my paper slippers scuffing the tile floor.

"Would you like to have dinner with me?" he asks.

"Sure."

"I'll pick you up at your hotel at eight o'clock." He looks at his watch. "I have a meeting with my managers now."

I'm confused. "My hotel in Osaka? We checked out this morning."

"Your hotel here. Everything has been arranged."

"I have to be back in Kyoto to teach tomorrow morning."

"Everything is arranged." He bows low. "Please say goodbye to Hermiko for me." He disappears around the corner.

—

Hermiko sprawls across my bed. The mini-bar door is ajar, she's uncorked the Rémy Martin and swigs from the bottle. Knocking the lid off a shoebox she takes out a pair of silver elf boots. "I don't remember buying these."

"You didn't. I bought them for you while you were trying on the transparent car coat with the Desiderata printed across the back."

"Louise, you're so sweet." She sits up and slips her bare feet into the supple boots. "They're perfect. Usually I'm hard to fit—my ankles are so thick."

Right. "What about this?" I turn from the mirror so she can get a better look at the dress I found on the Omote-Sando. Not a *number* like the one we bought in Kyoto, just a simple 150,000-yen frock of fluted gray silk crepe.

"I don't know"—she takes another pull at the cognac—"there's such a thing as too simple, too classic. With all that curly hair you risk looking like a Corinthian column. Try it with this." She sails a plum velvet bolero through the air.

"It will never fit me."

"I bought it for you while you were trying on hats."

"You're a pal, Hermiko." The bolero fits, and pushes my tits together and up in the bargain. "What do you think?"

She stretches and yawns. "Just the thing. I'm going to have a short nap. It's amazing how shopping wears one down."

"Oro said he'd be by at eight."

She doubles up a pillow and wedges it under her head. "I'm not sure I should go. He wants to see you, Louise."

"He's your friend—I'm the one who's tagging along."

She pulls a second pillow over her head. "Wake me at a quarter to."

—

The lobby has a swimming pool in it. You come out of the elevator onto a ramp that curves around a cylindrical glass tank. A Japanese boy in a shiny black thong glides underwater by my side as I lope down the ramp.

At the bottom there's a lounge filled with curving black leather benches. I look about for a trench-coated bodyguard. The benches are empty except for a long-haired guy in wire-rimmed glasses and a wispy goatee reading *Abitare*.

"Hello, Louise," he says.

"Oro."

"You did not recognize me." He gets up and, instead of bowing, stands on tiptoe to kiss my cheek. The hem of his black raincoat touches the marble floor.

"No."

He looks extremely pleased with himself. "Good."

"Hermiko will be right down."

"Hermiko?" He tilts his head to one side as though he can barely remember who this might be. "Do you like this hotel?"

"Yeah, it's pretty neat."

All of a sudden the drawbridge is up. When I walked into the lounge he was lighted from within—open house. Strange cat. What did I do wrong?

"Oro-*san!*" Hermiko flies down the ramp on silver elf boots.

"Hermiko-*san.*" His bow is low but jerky. Curt.

"Where are we going?" she asks.

"A restaurant not so far from here." He heads for the glass doors that give onto the street without waiting to see if we follow.

"Some disguise," Hermiko whispers to me. The doors glide open and we follow him out onto the sidewalk.

"Hey, look, it's Fu Manchu!" A mob of American sailors pause to give Oro the once-over, then saunter along the street guffawing over the little Jap in the big black coat.

Oro doesn't seem to have noticed, although his face has gone almost as dark as his coat. We follow him single file along the narrow sidewalk, dodging Western tourists and groups of Japanese businessmen already roseate with drink.

"Does this part of Tokyo have a name?" I call to Oro.

"Roppongi," he says, not bothering to turn around. He hurries on, his coat billows out behind him.

He stops in front of a slab of black marble into which has been set a narrow black glass door. "This is the place. You must excuse me, I have a very bad headache. I feel I must go home rather than spoil your evening. Please, you will dine as my guests. The reservation is under the name Mr. Dean."

He's gone before I can think of anything to say.

Hermiko and I stand together and stare at our reflections in the black marble.

—

We sit in a vinyl-covered booth in a basement barbecued-chicken joint, studying the flocked velvet menus. That marble-slab place where Oro had reservations looked like it would demand more than it offered and I for one didn't feel up to the challenge. In fact, I felt like I had just been slapped in the face and didn't know what for. But, I reminded myself, this is a foreign place and, despite the humiliation tingling my cheeks, it's hard to be sure. About anything. Hermiko's not saying much so I decide to test out my hypothesis. "Was that fucking rude or what?"

She doesn't look up from her menu. "What?"

"What he did."

"Oh"—she smiles to herself, as if remembering something—"you get used to that."

"I don't get used to that. He invites us out to dinner and then dumps us. And who's this Mr. Dean anyway?"

More to her menu than to me Hermiko says, "James Dean."

"Right. Oro's four feet tall, spends most of his life bowing—a real *Rebel Without a Cause* kind of guy."

She closes her menu. "He has permission to be rude, to be a renegade."

"Bet he even jaywalks."

Hermiko gives me a blank look as the waitress approaches. "Do you know what you want?"

"I guess I'll go for the baby back ribs and a side order of ginger tofu."

She relays our orders to the waitress, whose dress is of the same burgundy flocking as the menus. "It was my fault. I oughtn't to have come along."

"Why the hell not?"

"He wanted to see you, Louise."

The waitress returns to plunk down two plastic lacquer bowls of multicolored coleslaw.

"Why couldn't he have just said that?"

"That would have been rude. If you knew what he wanted, why did he need to say anything at all?"

"I thought he had permission to be a rebel."

She gives me a look that I see here a lot and am only just beginning to understand. What it says is: Even if I explain you will never understand for you are not Japanese. What she says is: "Speaking your mind isn't considered rebellious here, just stupid."

My mouth is full of the sweetest slaw I've ever tasted. "It's so fucking frustrating."

"I know." She lays her hand over mine. "May I speak frankly?"

"I wish someone would."

"I'm not sure you grasp the situation."

"What situation?"

"Becoming involved with Oro."

"Who says I'm involved?"

She picks up her plastic chopsticks, lays them down again. "There is little point in playing naive. I saw how you behaved during his concert, I saw how he looked at you backstage. You signaled your readiness and he picked you out."

"I'm supposed to be flattered?"

"You can be whatever you like."

"Are you fucking him, Hermiko?"

She tries to look shocked but can't help laughing. "We do not ask such questions in Japan."

"You *are* fucking him."

"We are like brother and sister."

"Who fuck."

"Louise! I would think Oro is fucking many people, whomever he likes."

"Boy after my own heart."

"But if you choose him and he chooses you, you will then not have so many choices."

"You said he can do whatever he wants."

"You have your ideas of freedom. They don't apply here. He's a little god with a lot of power. But his fans, all the people who grant him that power ... he is their nourishment as well."

"You're warning me off him."

"If you accept Oro, you also accept his story. His myth. You become a character in his drama."

I slap the table with one hand and laugh out loud. The plastic lacquer bowls jump and clatter. "Tell me something I don't know. He's such a little drama queen. A star. I've been in theater long enough to recognize the type, Hermiko. Toronto is full of stars. I just want to do him, not become a permanent part of the constellation."

She gives a slight bow. "I am so pleased you have clarified your position."

You bet. Maybe she's just mystified that her perfect little god is attracted to a woman big enough to swallow him whole. So join the club. I don't get it either. He's perfection and I'm ...well, I'm Louise, the girl with cheese between her knees. Maybe he figures the contrast will set him off to greater advantage. Like he needs it. Most of the time I try not to think about what's happening at all. I'm a girl who follows her cunt. You sort the rest out later.

Hermiko taps a silvered nail on the Formica tabletop. "Louise, where have you gone?"

"I'm right here."

"The waitress wants to know if there's something wrong with the ribs."

I look up at the flocked waitress's inquiring face. How long has she been standing there? "Tell her everything is *genki-genki*, my eyes were just bigger than my stomach." The waitress shrugs her shoulders and bears my full plate away.

"You seemed so far away." Hermiko's fingertips touch mine. "So sad."

"Sad? I don't think so. Just a little tired." When I'm sad I'll be the first to let her know, thank you very much.

—

The phone rings in the middle of my blacked-out hotel room in the middle of the blacked-out night in the middle of my blacked-out dreams. The red numbers on the digital clock say 3:14.

"Please," says a soft female voice, "you have a telephone call."

This usually is the case when the telephone rings.

A synthesizer plunks out the opening notes of "Send in the Clowns."

"Hello, this is Oro speaking."

"Oro, it's the middle of the bloody night."

"You are sleeping."

"No, I'm talking on the bloody phone."

"I need to talk to you."

"You could have done that earlier, at the restaurant, Mr. Dean."

"You are very angry at me, Louise?"

"Fucking straight I'm angry at you."

"'Fucking straight,'" he murmurs, savoring it. "I am so sorry. I wanted to see you so much, but only you. Understand? No Hermiko—I see Hermiko all the time. She is like my sister."

His voice is so low in his throat I have to listen closely just to get it all. Actors know this trick: you've got them on the edge of their seats if they're worried they can't quite hear you. There's also a purr to it—no, that would be too easy—a low buzz that vibrates through me. Against my will and better judgment I sigh, "I understand."

What's the point of arguing with him, or telling him off, or trying to make him feel rotten about what he pulled? Nothing will work against perfect all-devouring self-love. He's an *actor*, for fuck's sake, he will feign whatever I need. The most transparent man I have ever met. This is not nothing, is it?

"Louise?" Still there. I hadn't forgotten he was at the other end of the line but the sound of his breathing had mesmerized me.

"Yes, Oro?"

"I want to see you."

"Now? Where are you?"

"On the roof."

"Of my hotel?"

He giggles.

"No. I'm sleeping."

"Tomorrow? *Please?*"

"I'm going back to Kyoto tomorrow. Your helicopter is flying me there, very early in the morning. I have to work tomorrow."

"Me too. You are free tomorrow evening?"

"Let me consult my agenda."

He waits. I listen to another few bars of his breathing.

"I think I can fit you in. After work."

"I can come for dinner?"

"No!" We're not going to begin with me cooking for him. "Come after dinner. Around ten."

"Thank you, Louise. Sayonara."

Sayonara. Oh, fuck it. I mean, really.

—

Didn't get back to sleep. Or did. Didn't *feel* like sleep, but must have been, at least a second here, a millisecond there, long enough to have infolded my traveling dream. Don't know why I call it that, since no traveling occurs. I *prepare* to travel, half a dozen suitcases open across the pushed-together twin beds, taxi honking down in the street. The driver honks and honks in the night and I am nowhere ready. Can't find my shoes, or find them and they're caked with mud, or one heel's coming off. Can't find my favorite skirt, best dress, sheerest panties, or can find them and they're buttonless, torn, stained. I trundle up and down the corridor that bisects the apartment searching for needle and thread, spot remover, a traveling toaster that plugs into the cigarette lighter of my car, as if I ever had a car. Again and again the horn sounds and I, not out of sadness or anything pathetic like that, but out of pure frustration, start to cry. Not only my eyes, but every orifice. My nipples run with tears.

I awake, dry. Disappointed but relieved by my continence. Know I had the dream because it's all starting up again. And I'm not ready. Even if I were, it's not as if a thing like this is ever going to go right. I should leave—the horn is honking—but I can't.

From twelve or thirteen—let's be honest here—from two or three, I knew where love leads. Hungry looks and hot hands, unspeakable pleasure followed by unfathomable emptiness. They want, you want, the same things, different things, all at once, their dreams as richly tinctured as your own, but not—never—your own. You meet on a plain that tilts and fades even as you inhabit it, this fleshly equilibrium irrigated by hope and lies. At the beginning it's impossible not to see the end rise up in the distance. I would tell him stay away, if there were a voice to say it in. Thought I had climbed free of all of that. After the aptly named Peter, his sudden retreat, my protracted stay at the Red River Home for the Perplexed, I thought I would never go to that place again. Sex, yes, of course sex, flying fucks to keep the pipes in pitch. But never more than that. No intersection, no meeting of two sweating greedy souls. Separate is the way, alone is always preferable to … Let's just say that I am partial to any isolation that protects me from the gaudy losses of love.

14

The helicopter sets us down in the Heartful Purity parking lot a little after six. Hermiko and I clamber out. Grit flies up in our faces, stings our legs as we struggle with the shopping bags and boxes of Tokyo booty. We bypass the main gate and hurry along the narrow dirt path that follows the compound wall. This seems needlessly furtive since the girls must still be on cleaning detail at this hour, but Hermiko leads the way. And if we are seen, so what? The School of Heartful Purity's a pink prison for them not us.

She leaves me at the gate that leads to my bungalow. From the gravel walk I can see that the front shoji screens are open a crack. I step onto the veranda, slide them back and, kicking off my shoes, step onto the tatami.

There in the middle of the table is the largest cantaloupe I've ever seen—smaller than a globe of the world but bigger than a soccer ball. Holy smokes, I am the recipient of a gift fruit. Isn't that sweet of him. Picture one of the trenchcoat guys sneaking into the Heartful Purity compound, a big melon tucked under one beefy arm. I sit at the low table and stare at the pale goosefleshed skin. The place feels damp. Reaching under the *kotatsu* table, I switch on the radiant lamp that is the bungalow's sole source of warmth. Autumn's coming. I give the melon a good thump, it sounds dark and dense.

My nearly sleepless night has left me strangely clear-headed. I sit at the table a while longer, prodding the cantaloupe so it wobbles a little this way, a little that, nudge it toward the edge, at the last minute rolling it back to safety. The killer inside me wants to snatch it up, haul it outside and give it a big basketball heave into the compound wall, watch the moist flesh slide slowly down. But I should go for breakfast—serving stops in seven minutes. Can't seem to tear myself away from the table. Is it the spreading warmth of the *kotatsu* lamp or the cantaloupe's gravity that holds me down?

I get up and go for the cleaver that hangs, along with the other kitchen utensils I never use, over the two-burner mini-stove. I slide Friday's *Japan Times* under the cantaloupe and bring the cleaver down with a satisfying thwack, neatly slicing through rind, flesh and pulp. Seeds fly everywhere, one sticks to my cheek like a lacquer beauty mark. The fruity odor spills out in a rich sweet wave. I scoop out the remaining seeds from the bowl of each hemisphere with my fingers, making a fist each time to let the warm juice squish out the cracks before plopping the seeds onto the paper. The golden flesh is so soft and tender I can scoop it up too, stuffing my mouth so full the juice runs down my chin, streaks my neck and plasters my shirt against my tits.

After gorging on the melon I fell asleep, head on table. When I awoke it was after eight. Picked the seeds out of my hair, changed into teacher clothes, brushed my furry teeth. I'm tearing along the corridor that leads to my classroom when Madame Watanabe veers around the corner. She too is running, in that way Japanese women have perfected: upper body held stiff and upright—see, I do not run at all—while feet and ankles are a blur of movement like the paws of that little dog in the Futurist painting. She skids to a halt and bows.

"Your class waiting waiting."

"Thank you so much for keeping an eye on them, Madame Watanabe. I was delayed."

She readjusts her clump of black hair, which has subsided over one eye. "Delay no good for Heartful Purity students. Teacher set example. Not bad example. Good one."

"I'm late because Mr. Arakawa wanted to see me." This is mildly true. Arakawa asked to see me Friday before class—I was late then too.

"Oh, Arakawa-*san*." Madame Watanabe bows until the sleeves of her shiny black gown—like a cross between a silk parachute and a garbage bag—touch the salmon-carpeted floor. "He tell you what you do wrong?"

"Not exactly."

"New teacher need guidance, always guidance, specially *gaijin* teacher, ignorant of Japan way."

"Mr. Arakawa told me he was very happy with my teaching."

Madame Watanabe smiles. "Very polite man, Arakawa-*san*."

"He asked me if I'd like to prepare a short musical show with my students. Something in English, to perform just for the school."

"Ah." Madame Watanabe's smile stretches her face out of shape, pale gums so receded that her great horse teeth hang on by the tips of the roots. "He ask me same thing. What show you do? Not much with only six girls, I bet. *Sonnamusic? Ne*, too big. *Okrahoma?* No good either. What you do?"

Fuck if I know. I had intended to think about it over the weekend, but Oro intervened. "It's a secret," I say. "Something original."

"Original." The concept is too much for her. "You write music, word, lyric, everything? You very talent." She turns to go.

"Not just me. My students and I will do it together. They're very creative, you know."

"Creative," she spits out. "Not here to create, here to learn."

I sail serenely past her. "We learn through creating, Madame Watanabe." She mutters something I don't get. I turn. "What?"

She smoothes down her shiny gown with black lacquer talons. "The Imaginary Theater Company of Toronto. You create like that?"

I stand stock-still. "That's right."

"I call directory assistance, Toronto. No number for Imaginary Theater Company."

Evil bitch. "We're on hiatus."

"What that?"

"Taking a break. We lost our funding so we had to close the office temporarily." Half of me wants to yell out, "There is no telephone because the Imaginary Theater Company is imaginary, you old sow." Instead I take a leaf from Hermiko's book of manners and bow low to Madame Watanabe.

She steps back, looking confused.

"Madame Watanabe, we must get to know each other better. I'd like to tell you more about the Imaginary Theater Company and I'd like to know more about you as well. I'm sure we have a lot of knowledge to share. And a woman of your age ... well, you have so much more experience than I do. I'd be interested in hearing about *your* dramatic training, if any."

It's her turn to bow. "We do soon."

———

Throw open the classroom door, catch the girls in mid-flight. Keiko pinwheels about the room, arms held out stiff, parallel to the floor. Michiko, Noriko, Fumiko and Hideko run after her, leap from cushion to cushion, all of them droning, "*Mokka-mokka-mokka, mokka-mokka-mokka.*" Akiko, ever the class monitor, stands to one side, arms akimbo, observing. She notices me first, then the others. Keiko spins on, oblivious.

"What's going on?" I kick cushions out of the way and stand in the middle of the room. Keiko sees me now but continues madly spinning. She whirls about me so her fingertips nearly graze my cheeks.

"Keiko crazy," Michiko reports, tearing away a strip of cuticle. As if she hadn't been flying about the room moments before. "You want me to stop her?"

"If she's crazy you can't stop her. She'll just spin on and on and on until she turns into butter."

"Butter?" Fumiko says. "Now you who crazy."

"'Is'—'is crazy,' Fumiko."

"I is crazy," Noriko says with a laugh. Soon they're all repeating it, except for class monitor Akiko, whose face can't unfrown itself, and Keiko, who shows no sign of winding down.

"Keiko is only imitating," Hideko explains as she tugs a knee sock higher up one plump leg.

"Imitating what, Hideko? A dervish, a windmill, a top, a—"

"Helicopter!" Keiko shouts and stops spinning. Her grin couldn't be wider. "Teacher come to school in helicopter."

This sets them off again. Even scared little Michiko holds her arms out straight and joins the spinning chorus. *"Mokka-mokka-mokka, mokka-mokka-mokka."*

Akiko hurries after them, a finger to her lips, making shushing noises, but they pay her no mind.

"I was away for the weekend."

"Where you away?" Fumiko insists.

"I went to Osaka and then to Tokyo to … to do some shopping."

"Shopping!" Hideko's chubby face lights up.

"You go shopping in helicopter?" Noriko says, nudging Fumiko.

"I went on a train but came back in a whirlybird."

"Whirlybird?" Michiko bites her lower lip.

"Mokka-mokka-mokka," Fumiko mutters to Noriko.

"Who helicopter?" Keiko wants to know.

"A friend of Hermiko's."

"Rich friend," Hideko sighs.

"I really think we should get started now." It's like being back in fucking Lethbridge, so tight and small everyone knows everything before it happens. "We're running late."

Fumiko won't let it drop. "Who helicopter?"

I could fix her up with a good plastic surgeon, take care of the mole and sew up the mouth too, no extra charge.

"Gift for you when you come back," Noriko chimes in. "On table."

Keiko glides very close and murmurs in my ear, "*Mokka-mokka.*"

That does it. I grab her arm and push her down onto a cushion. It slides away and her bum hits the floor. Michiko yelps as though I'd pushed *her* down. Akiko wrings her hands.

"Everyone shut the fuck up and sit down, OK?"

Michiko plumps down on the nearest cushion, a handful of fingers in her mouth. Noriko, Akiko and Hideko follow suit. Only Fumiko takes her sweet time, pushing her cushion this way and that with one stockinged toe until she gets it exactly where she wants it, between Noriko's cushion and Keiko's, which remains unoccupied as Keiko has chosen to remain on the floor.

"I am your teacher but this does not mean that I belong to you. There's nothing I can do to stop you spying on me"— Michiko hangs her head—"at the same time, I have the right to a private life. What I do on my downtime is none of your bloody business, understand?"

Long silence.

Finally Hideko, chipmunk cheeks blushing, says, "Not spying."

"No, never spying," Akiko adds. "It was our morning to trim the bushes of the chess game next to the parking lot."

"But how did you know about my gift fruit? Someone has been snooping around inside my house."

It's Keiko's turn to hang her head.

"This has got to stop. How would you like it if I invaded your privacy? Wouldn't that bother you?"

The girls who aren't studying the floor look at me and shake their heads.

"It wouldn't bother you?"

Michiko raises her hand uncertainly.

"You don't need to do that, Michiko. Just talk."

"No private life in Japan."

"What's that supposed to mean?"

Michiko raises her head to look at me, tears in her eyes. "It's true. Everyone part of everyone else. We all a part together, like big family. No single part."

Clear as mud. "So anyone has the right to walk into my house and poke around?"

Keiko stares into my eyes. "No, that wrong. Most of time. Someone have very good reason, maybe OK. But you right—wrong to go into house."

"And my private life—my weekends—are not my own?"

Akiko says, "You are a part of us now, we are a part of you. Everyone pull together." She must have been a cheerleader in a former life.

"For the school," Fumiko and Noriko recite together, "everyone for the school."

"School more important," Hideko says, interlacing sausage fingers to illustrate, "than me or you or anyone."

"Look, I'm for the school too, but my weekends are my own. Got it?"

They look sideways at one another as if to say, what's the use, she'll never understand. And they're right: I don't want to know. All I want is my weekends and my privacy.

"Got it?" I repeat and wait silently until they all, even sulky Keiko, nod their heads. "Keiko, move back onto your cushion; your bum's going to get cold."

"Bum?" Keiko says.

I point to my own. "Butt. Glutes. Ass. Arse. Buns. Bottom. Behind. Sweetcheeks. Buttocks. Rear. Posterior. Backside. Rump. Hind. Hunkers. Fanny. Stern. Tail. Tush."

"Tush." Noriko starts laughing and can't stop.

Keiko slips back onto her cushion and flashes me a look from under black bangs.

"What we need to talk about now is what kind of show we want to put on. Mr. Arakawa says it shouldn't be too long or elaborate, and that we can use one of the big rehearsal rooms three days a week."

"We put on real show?" Michiko says.

"One performance only, for the school, in Cocoon Hall."

"Cocoon Hall," Hideko sighs.

"What kind of show is what we have to decide. Do we want to do a musical, or at least part of a musical like—I don't know—*West Side Story* or *Cabaret*, or do we want to come up with a show of our own?"

"*West Side Story*," Noriko says and launches into a passable imitation of Rita Moreno. "'A boy like that wants one thing only, and when he's done he'll leave you lonely ..."'

"*Dr. Dolittle*," Hideko says.

"That would be hard—all those animal costumes."

"*Mary Poppins*," Akiko our own personal nanny says.

Without looking up, Keiko sings in a mournful alto, "'Feed the birds, tuttance a bag ...'"

"We do something our own?" Michiko says without raising her hand. "What you mean?"

"We make up the story and the songs and the dance numbers and everything."

"Like what?" Fumiko wants to know.

How about The Story of the Mole Princess? "It could be a myth or a fairy tale or a story from history, or even something from your own lives."

"Our lives nothing interesting," Keiko says, chin in hands.

"But in English?" Hideko asks.

"It has to be in English but it could be a story about Japan."

"English class!" Akiko cries out. "We will make a musical about English class."

Oh God.

"Stupid idea," Keiko says.

"Boring," Noriko agrees.

Everyone thinks for a while, then Michiko says, "Izanagi and Izanami."

"Who?"

"Izanagi and Izanami. They brother-sister but marry too. When Izanami die Izanagi very sad. He go to Land of Yellow Stream to take her back."

The other girls nod. Excited, Noriko takes up the tale. "Gods of Yellow Stream say she go back with Izanagi but first must prepare for the journey. Gods tell Izanagi, stay outside, wait for your sister."

"He waits and waits," Akiko continues in a singsong schoolmistress voice. "Izanami takes a long time to pack—she can't find her favorite kimono, her servant has to finish pressing the obi. Then Izanagi can wait no longer. He crashes into Yellow Stream Palace and finds the room where Izanami stays."

She pauses, everyone sits in perfect silence. They know how it ends but savor it not ending yet.

"She dead." Keiko's voice is flat. "Izanagi find her rotten body, covered with bugs. What you call fat white bugs who eat dead?"

"Maggots."

"Maggots? Izanami wear maggot kimono," Keiko says and laughs softly.

Make a hell of a musical.

"Gods of death," Michiko adds in a tremulous voice, "chase Izanagi, want to keep him in Land of Yellow Stream. He throws peaches at them, they stop to eat, he fly away." More gift fruit.

"We have a story like that in the West too, about a guy named Orpheus whose wife dies and he goes to the underworld to bring her back, but he screws up too and she dies a second time, just like Izanami. Are there any cheerful Japanese legends? Or at least without maggots?"

"Fox wedding," Fumiko says. Noriko claps her hands joyously at this suggestion. "Little boy's mother," Fumiko begins, "say, 'Rain, sunshine same time—today foxes' wedding. At end of rainbow in forest. You stay inside.' Little boy go into forest, quiet-quiet, watches foxes' wedding. When he come home, his mother lock up house, no let him in."

"*Won't* let him in, Fumiko. What happens to the little boy?"

Fumiko thinks a moment. "I think he die. Very small boy."

"What about you, Louise?" Keiko says. This is the first time any of them has used my first name. Till now it's always been "teacher" or "Miss Painchaud." "Do you know story we could use?"

"I don't know. There is one that occurred to me, except I don't know what you'd think of it. It's half-Japanese, half-*gaijin*, about a lady from the West who falls in love with a Japanese man."

I can see they're hooked already.

—

The moon, a slice less than full, hangs over the valley, a peach about to fall. Teapot hot in one hand, ceramic cup cool in the other, I step barefoot out onto the veranda. The soft wind sifts through the pines. I sit down on the moon-washed boards and, pretending to be what I am not, place pot and cup just so. Sit back on my heels to admire the effect, then arrange the crockery twice more.

"Louise."

He crouches against the wall, knees drawn up to his chin.

"Fucking hell, Oro. You could at least knock or something, let a girl know you're here."

"I wanted to surprise you."

"You did that all right. How'd you find your way into the compound?" The gift fruit wobbles through my mind. "But of course, you or one of your minions already knew the way."

He looks at me like I'm speaking a foreign language. Which I am. The harvest moon shines in his pupils, tiny gold coins.

"How was your day?" He gets up from his crouch, bowing as he rises. His oversized black sweater hangs down past his knees, long sleeves obscuring small hands.

"My day was a joy from end to end, Oro. How about yours?"

"Boring. Disgusting. Very hard."

"You're shooting a film?"

"In Kamakura. Do you know this city?"

I shake my head.

"A very old city. We are filming an old drama—from the sixteenth century. With heavy historical costumes. All day long I wear a big hat and a long sword that scrapes against my side."

"What is it called?"

"Sorry?"

"What is the film's title?"

"*Ano* ... in English it would be very hard to say. It is a long title, a famous samurai story. I will try: 'He Goes After His Friend to the Other World After Torturing Him to Death.'"

Yet another possibility for a rollicking Japanese musical. "You play a samurai who tortures his best friend to death and then follows him to the underworld?"

His eyes close as if he's watching the whole bloody saga play across the insides of his eyelids. "Very sad."

"Most love stories are." I get up. "Let me fetch you a teacup."

Motioning for me to stay where I am he goes over to where he had been crouching and returns with a silver bottle of sake, the largest I've ever seen. "I believe you like sake, Louise?"

"Does the pope shit in the woods?"

"I am sorry?"

"Yes, I like sake."

"You like many things Japanese."

I recite the obligatory *gaijin* list: "I like sushi and chopsticks and green tea. I like Mishima and moonwatching and snowflakes on mittens."

He holds up a finger. "I have one thing Japanese that you do not know, but I am sure you will like."

"Oh?"

"Almost sure." He digs deep into the pockets of his jeans and comes up with a round silver pillbox inlaid with dark jade.

"Are we going to do Serenity?" I try to keep the greed out of my voice.

He looks at me. "Serenity? That is last year's drug. No one takes Serenity any more."

Excuse my provincialism.

He opens the pillbox: two transparent capsules on green velvet.

"What are these called?"

"Emptiness."

"Emptiness?"

"One pill makes you feel one way, a different pill makes you feel another way. This can be very boring, I find. Disgusting. With Emptiness you feel nothing."

I think I follow. "And we wash it down with sake?" I pick up the bottle, which is icy. "I'll go warm this up. You think we'll kill the whole bottle?"

He takes it from my hands. "This we drink cold."

"Cold sake?"

"It is delicious cold. Very special sake. It comes from the island where I was born—Shodoshima in the Inland Sea."

"I'll get another cup."

He picks up mine. "This is enough. We will drink from the same cup."

Would I be disappointed if I ever met an actor who *wasn't* a romantic, or would my soul clap hands and sing?

He pours the cup to the brim, hands it to me. The cheap ceramic glows in the moonlight. "Open your mouth, please." He places the capsule on the tip of my tongue. "Now drink."

No kidding, boyo. I toss it back. Cold and dry, almost tasteless. Then my mouth floods with silver. I hand him the empty cup. "Excellent stuff. Where can I buy a barrel?"

"This sake is not for sale. I will bring you many bottles, Louise." He replenishes the cup and washes down his capsule.

"How long does it take to work?"

"Emptiness? You touch it with your tongue, it starts to work right away."

Oh. Then this is it. I don't feel a thing. Subtle Japanese joke? "No, really, when does it start to work?"

"I told you—now. It is working now."

I'm determined not to say it. Then I do. "I don't feel a thing."

"You like?"

"How can I like it if I can't feel it?"

He smiles and with one finger touches my lower lip. "You feel Emptiness."

"I've been feeling that all my life, Oro."

He laughs, claps his hands. Funny Louise. "Not *that*. That's not real Emptiness."

"No," I agree, "that's terror and panic, anxiety, abject misery, family values."

"A lot of things."

"Yeah."

"You feel these things now?"

"I don't think so."

"You feel anything?"

"Silver. Clear."

He claps small hands once more. "That's it!"

I would laugh except there's no need to. No desire to either. There is just me, upright on these silvered boards, Oro opposite, taking off his enormous sweater.

"It is warm for autumn." A warm breeze, on cue, ruffles my curls. His sleeveless black undershirt has a zip down the front. His bare arms are thin and small-muscled, like a boy's. This in fact is what he looks like, skin almost blue in the pale light: a thirteen-year-old boy.

I feel nothing, tears roll down my cheeks.

He rubs them away with the heels of his hands. "This happens sometimes. It is part of Emptiness, Louise."

Takes a long time to empty me out. Good at waiting, Oro. Sits with feet tucked under him. When I'm all done he takes my face in his hands and licks away the salt. I know this is something he has done in a movie or on a TV show or maybe in a curry commercial, and I don't care. There is nothing to care about. A boy licks my face, I am a child molester—thoughts, impressions, sensations click through my mind like billiard balls across spotless felt and dunk into pockets so deep as to be irretrievable. In the next valley or the next, a train whistle blows.

I reach for the zip of his undershirt and give it a tug. It splits open down to his thick black belt. A polished silver scar runs like a second zip from his sternum down almost to his belly button. I trace it with one finger. It's cool, compared to the rest of his skin.

"What's this scar?"

He looks into my eyes. "Highway to my heart."

So be inscrutable. He is so thin and small, he is so beautiful, he is so warm in my hands, which nearly span his waist. And I am so ... so ...

I am so fucking huge. For an instant I see how I must appear to him, as if he is an explorer in a small barque and I am his New Found Land. I jump to my feet, knock over the sake cup.

"Louise, what are you doing?"

Looking down at him, I strip the undershirt all the way off. "You want a ride?"

"Yes, please."

"Stand up." I hold my arms out before me, parallel to the floor. He falls prone across them. Weighs about as much as a sheaf of bamboo. Twice as fragrant. "Ready?"

"Yes."

Spin him round and round and round. At first silent, only the slap of my feet on the bare boards, my breath rasps louder the more I turn, heartbeat in my ears. I open my mouth to whoop and music pours out. Three voices, female voices, none of them my own, intertwine like silver currents in a fast cold stream.

15

Keiko plumps the cushion next to hers, inviting me to sit down.

To sit down is to stop. I don't want to stop. The three singing voices tumble through my head. Why shouldn't it be like last night forever? Yet the very concept—*forever*—makes me gag. Why is there so much absence this morning? Is anything more humiliating than becoming a romantic sap?

"Let me try to give you the bare bones of the story I was telling you about last class."

"Bare bones?" Fumiko says.

"Like Japanese saying?" Michiko wants to know. "'Even a beauty in the morning turns to bones in the evening—the world is changing without end.'"

"'Bare bones' means the story's basic outline, its plot. A *gaijin* lady comes to work in Japan, she falls in love with a Japanese man who, uh, works in the arts. They know that what's happening between them is basically a one-night stand"—I pause, thinking I'll have to explain, but everyone seems to get it—"the lady has to go back to her country at some point, the man has his real life in Japan. Because their meeting is so brief and the circumstances impossible, their love becomes stronger, more passionate. The more they see they won't have it, the more they want it. They also want it because it is so unlike anything either of them has ever known, because it exists outside either person's real world. It takes place in secret, in stolen time, in exotic places."

"But what is important is that they love," Keiko says, her eyes boring into mine.

"I'm not even sure it's that. Maybe the most important thing is that they're both foreigners."

"You said he is Japanese," Fumiko reminds me, "not foreign."

"He is foreign to her, as foreign as she is to him. Each is the other's unknown. Each one wants—"

"This why so exciting!" Keiko says, rubbing her thighs.

"The question is"—they turn toward me, open-mouthed —"can we make a musical out of this, or is the material too thin?"

"Very beautiful," Michiko says. "Very sad."

"Love story always work." Keiko strokes the empty pillow at her side. "Simple is best."

"The way I see it, this is essentially a two-hander: female lead, male lead, with lots of doubling in the incidental roles—passersby, a waiter in a restaurant, strangers in a train station, a bartender, that kind of thing. Obviously Keiko will play the Japanese man."

Keiko bows her head and struggles not to look pleased.

"But who will play the *gaijin* lady?" I look them over,

trying to determine who would be most convincing in a "Western" role. Noriko might be able to pull it off, except she's feminine in such a tremulous Japanese way. Michiko has the emotional intensity, but she's so shy. Akiko, with the soul and smile of a kindergarten teacher, is impossible. And Hideko's too rotund.

"You, Louise," Keiko says. "You play *gaijin*."

"Because I smell like one?"

Keiko hops to her feet and stands facing me. "See, perfect. I little bit short—wear tall shoes for show. Just right." She places her hands on my shoulders and looks into my eyes. "Perfect romantic couple."

I remove her hands from my shoulders. "I don't think so, Keiko. For one thing, I can't carry a tune in a bucket. For another, she's meant to be a beautiful *gaijin* lady, so beautiful the Japanese man thinks about giving up everything he has in order to be with her."

Michiko and Keiko exchange looks.

"Michiko, why are you and Keiko grinning like that?"

"You beautiful," Keiko says, eyes bright.

"Man do anything for you," Michiko says. "Special man."

"*Mokka-mokka-mokka*," Keiko whispers.

"I think we're getting a little ahead of ourselves here. We don't even have a script yet. I thought today we should try some warm-up exercises, just to get us started."

"Exercises?" Keiko drops to the floor and executes a dozen push-ups, narrow biceps bulging.

"Let's go to the rehearsal room so we'll have space to move around in." They scramble to their feet. "Bring your cushions with you."

We tear along the corridor. Michiko balances her cushion on her head. Noriko sits on hers, Fumiko pulls it like a sled. Keiko lightly thwacks the back of my head with hers. Akiko tries to bring up the rear in proper monitor style, but Hideko's ambulation is stately and unhurried, as befits her size.

I start to open the door to Small Rehearsal Room B. A scatting Sarah Vaughan stops me. Through the small window in the door I can see Madame Watanabe swoop about the room like a demented crow, long sleeves of her black pajamas flying. The Dirt Troupe girls follow close behind. Orange papier mâché beaks obscure their faces, black feathers cover their arms.

I usher my class into Small Rehearsal Room A. Noriko goes over to the piano and plunks out "Love Is a Many Splendored Thing" while Keiko hovers ever closer to me.

"Cut it out, Keiko. Kill the piano, Noriko. Let's get down to business."

"Down to business," Akiko echoes, careful to brush off her cushion before sitting down.

On the blackboard I draw a vertical line and write JAPANESE on one side and GAIJIN on the other. "First I thought we should concentrate on what it means to be Japanese. Have you ever done any free-associating?"

Blank looks all around.

"I say a word, then you say the first word that comes into your mind. OK?"

Everyone nods. Noriko launches into a spirited rendition of "Chopsticks."

"Off the piano, Noriko. Now. Although maybe that's not a bad place to start. All right, 'chopsticks' is my first word."

Long silence as they all stare at me.

"That's not how it works. I say 'chopsticks' and you say the first word that comes to mind."

Another long silence.

"No, no, no. You can't think about it. It has to be spontaneous."

Nothing.

"I don't get it. What's so complicated about this?"

Noriko spins on the piano stool. "First you must say word."

"I did say it. Several times."

"But not by itself," Fumiko reminds me.

"Oh. OK. 'Chopsticks.'"

"Wood," Keiko cries.

"Paper."

"House," Akiko says.

"Fire."

"Pretty," Keiko says, then puts a hand over her mouth.

"Kimono."

"Doll," Hideko says.

"Woman."

"Doll," Hideko says again.

"Man."

"Father," Michiko yawns.

"Tokyo."

"Smelly." Akiko holds her nose.

"Polluted." Keiko coughs.

"Cockroaches," Hideko says, pursing plump lips.

"Cockroaches? Is that a problem in Tokyo?"

They all laugh now, sharing an uproarious private joke.

"Problem everywhere in Japan," Noriko offers.

More laughter.

"Really? How come I've never seen one?"

"You have," Keiko assures me. "Millions of them."

Hideko falls about on her cushion in spasms of laughter.

Michiko takes pity on my incomprehension. "Japanese people cockroaches." She wiggles her fingers like antennae. "All crowdy together, all hurry-hurry-hurry. Come out of train station like million cockroaches out of food closet. Japanese go everything in group, like cockroach go. Japanese take over whole world, like cockroach your apartment."

"Cockroaches! Cockroaches!" Fumiko and Noriko cry, wiggling fingers above their heads.

"Cockroaches!" Michiko shrieks and suddenly they form an undifferentiated bunch, packed together, and scurry madly about the rehearsal hall, fingers wiggling, all of them screaming, "Cockroach, cockroach, everybody cockroach!"

The door flies open. Madame Watanabe swoops in. My students swarm from one end of the room to the other, still screaming. Jostling behind Madame Watanabe, Dirt Troupe in full feather.

"What is meaning?" Madame Watanabe wants to know. "What is meaning?"

"Meaning, Madame Watanabe?"

"So noisy, Dirt Troupe no rehearse."

"I am so sorry." I bow till the blood runs to my head. "Girls," I call out, "we have a visitor."

They swarm back to me, fingers wiggling. Gathered around me they whisper, "Cockroaches-cockroaches-cockroaches."

"What are you rehearsing, Madame Watanabe?"

"'Lullaby of Birdland.'" Ranged behind her, Dirt Troupe softly caws.

"Sarah Vaughan," I say.

"Hard to hear, your class so noisy," Madame Watanabe says.

"What happened to *Cabin in the Sky*?"

Papier mâché beaks poke over her shoulders. "No good. Arakawa-*san* say, 'Interesting but no cigar.' Make new piece now."

"You're switching to jazz?"

"Only for overture, big opening number." Madame Watanabe strokes the feathers of the tallest member of Dirt Troupe. "You know Alfred Hitchcock movie *The Birds*?"

"You're making a musical out of that?"

Madame Watanabe nods. The tall girl leans over and pecks her lightly on the cheek. The cawing grows louder. A fluttering of wings. "What you rehearse?"

"We're not really rehearsing yet. Just doing improv exercises to loosen up a little."

Madame Watanabe smiles. "Something you learn at Imaginary Theater Company?"

"Warm-up exercises are important for—"

She surveys the students huddled around me. "They too loose already. Why they yell 'cockroach'?"

"To work on their r's, Madame Watanabe."

"I see." She folds voluminous sleeves across her chest. "They be very careful, your girls. Very very careful."

"Very careful about what?"

"They cockroaches, my birds come eat them, yop-yop."

"It was nice of you to drop by." I bow so close to her she has to back up or get beaned by my big noggin. Dirt Troupe caws in protest but backs away as well. I close the door behind them.

—

Step onto the veranda, shed my shoes, slide open the door. The table's covered with plastic shopping bags, flat boxes and round containers of various sizes, silver-labeled bottles of sake, two-liter aluminum canisters of Sapporo, two squat bottles of cognac. Someone has turned on the *kotatsu* lamp. I switch it off on the Canadian principle that if you start heating in October, what will you do when real winter comes?

Soft regular raspy noises from the bathroom. Push open the door. Oro, in a white loincloth with a red-and-white kamikaze band tied round his head, is down on his hands and knees, going at the pipes under the sink with a toothbrush and a teacup full of cleaning solvent. All the bathroom fixtures, right down to the chrome towel racks, have an unnatural luster. In the gathering dusk the toilet trough gleams spectrally on its tiled dais.

"Oro, what are you doing?"

He holds up the toothbrush and smiles. "We finished shooting early today—the set fell down. I am cleaning for you." Sweat and grit streak his golden chest.

"I can see that. A Heartful Purity cleaning lady comes by every second day to straighten up."

"She is not very good." With an open hand he indicates the whole room. "Very dirty."

"Thanks a bunch."

"Don't be angry. I like to clean for you. I am a tidy-up person."

"Oh?"

"Later I will polish all shoes."

"Oro, I—"

"First I must make dinner." I follow the damp triangle of his naked back into the main room where he turns up the *kotatsu*. "It's very cold," he says, hugging himself.

"All this food"—I open one of the shopping bags and take out a tubular tasseled object that may be a tuber—"it's enough for a week not a dinner."

"I failed to tell you? I have invited guests."

"You invited guests here? Who?"

"Big surprise." He washes his hands at the sink and goes over to the table where he unwinds a stretch of burgundy cloth from around a package about the size of a Monopoly game, strips off the pink swan-pattern wrapping paper underneath and peels away the gold foil beneath the pink paper to reveal a cling-wrapped box of sushi.

I survey the unopened cartons and canisters. "My kitchen facilities are pretty limited. There's no oven—just the two burners and the grill."

"Oven?" He turns to me laughing. "I don't cook, I open."

Once we have stripped away the layers and layers of decorative and protective wrapping, we're surrounded by food that either needs no cooking or has already been cooked: oysters lazing on pearly beds, skewered chicken parts in sesame sauce, shrimp tempura, pickled eel, pickled radishes, pickled turnip, pickled pickles, cold octopus soup, beef satay, pastel bean-curd petits fours, a mini-crate of round yellow pears and a box of ripe peaches.

"OK, time for bath," Oro says, standing on tiptoe to kiss my cheek.

"Not OK." I hold him suspended in place. He squirms warm and naked in my arms. "You stink."

"Stink? What does this mean?" His eyes are dark and wide.

"You smell. Very bad."

"Sorry." He hangs his head.

"I thought Japanese weren't supposed to smell." I burrow my nose into the tuft of hair under his arm. "Stinkola, baby."

"Disgusting," he whispers in my ear. "I am so very sorry."

"B.O. in a big way." I lick out his smelly salty pit.

"B.O.?"

"Body odor." With one hand I push cartons, boxes and bottles aside and lay him down on the wooden tabletop.

He looks up at me unsmiling. "Guests will arrive soon, Louise."

"Fuck 'em. They'll have to wait their turn."

"You are crazy."

"You bet I am." I insert a finger in his loincloth pouch. "And you're hard."

"Crazy girl."

Wrap my fingers around him and squeeze. With my index finger I smear the juice that trickles out all along the narrow shaft, then go back for more to wet his balls, small as cherries.

The aureoles of his nipples shine almost purple against his skin, the nipples themselves tiny dark cones. I taste one, then the other, sworl them with my tongue, bring my teeth into play. It's his turn to sing, high and true as a child. Until now I had no idea of his true range.

Flip him over on the hard tabletop and untangle the headband knot from the damp black hair that waves about the nape of his neck. "What are you doing?" his lips murmur to the tabletop. "What are you doing?"

"Crazy dirty things to smelly Japanese boy." I unknot the kamikaze cloth and wrap it round his narrow wrists, tying them tightly together at the base of his spine. The globes of his cheeks quiver and swell. The narrow vertical strip of his loincloth disappears between them.

Slap him lightly on one cheek, then the other. Pull out the strap of hidden cloth. It's damp, slightly discolored down the center, a streak of palest gold. Slap him again, harder. "Smelly dirty little boy."

"Sorry," he sighs. "I am so sorry."

They rise so firm and round to the palms of my hands, the flesh darkens and grows warmer with every blow. "Gift fruit," I whisper in his ear and enter him with one finger. He sings again, but lower. If someone were listening from the veranda it might sound like a groan. Only heat and softness now, liquid space and velvet walls, the anemone grip of him. Saliva strings down onto the tabletop from his parted lips. The song he sings is low and slow, a pleasure dirge. Slowly I slide out, as though uncorking a bottle of fine wine, then slide back in, two this time. His voice breaks, climbs higher. The deeper I probe, the higher it goes, his pelvis rising off the table. With my free hand check the loincloth pouch, the pulsing shaft and dripping head. It's now, the moment is here, to narrow my fingers together and scoop him out. The more I press in the more he pushes back until his body arches above the table, impaled, and he sings the last rippling notes, cheeks clutched round my hand, whole body straining. He spurts into my other hand until the pouch is drenched, my fingers coated.

He collapses. We are so still. The final note, a sostenuto sigh, comes eons later, as I withdraw.

—

They stand arrayed in the cool darkness of my veranda like a ready-made fashion spread. Five—no, six of them, the Tokyo boys I saw backstage at his concert in Osaka. They bow low, lots of creaking leather. The ones who aren't wearing leather jackets with shoulders out to here are wedged into leather jodhpurs and black lace-up boots with soles like hooves. They must all go to the same hairdresser, someone big on the tendrilled *fleur bleu* look—lots of loops and dips and spit curls. I can smell the mousse from here.

"Hey, guys. I'm Louise. Oro's still in the bath. You'd better come on in."

It takes some doing, and undoing, to get them from the veranda to the flagstoned entryway to the tatami mats. Lots of unbuckling, unzipping, unlacing, unfastening. One little guy—the rest of them are a lot taller than Oro—gets trapped in the cowl neck of his leather blouson and has to be wrestled out of it by the others.

Once on the tatami the bows begin all over again. Such white shirts they have—silk, satin, jersey, lisle, grosgrain, the little guy in shantung.

Two of them step forward. I know how it sounds when I say they all look alike, but you take a roomful of nineteen-year-old Japanese strangers, all of whom have the same hair and eye color, the same lithe bodies and flawless complexions, and see just how distinguishable they are. Anyway, these two guys look like all the others, but they also look more like each other than like the other four, so it dawns on me they may be twins.

"I am Kai," the one in the jersey body shirt announces, "and this"—he points to his *semblable* in the satin tunic—"is my brother Kei."

"I am so very pleased to meet you," Kei says, vigorously shaking my big hand with his two slender ones. "One has heard so much about you."

"Well, I hope you won't hold any of it against me."

I wait for the laugh. Could wait forever.

"Did you have trouble finding the place?"

Kai steps forward as the official spokesperson. "Not at all, thank you. Oro's driver dropped us off. He seemed to know the way."

Kei gives a hiccup of laughter and covers his face with his hands.

Kai introduces the rest: "Yasujiro, Nagisa, Masahiro and Steve."

"Steve," I say. "How'd you end up with a name like that?"

"Leeves Steve," the little guy says, thrusting out his chest.

"Steve Leaves—who's that?"

Kai interrupts. "Steve Reeves. Steve speaks no English, but he has named himself after the famous American actor, Steve Reeves."

"Steve Reeves," I say, thinking I've missed something in the translation.

"*Hercules Unchained,*" Kei says. "*The Last Days of Pompeii, The Giant of Marathon, The Trojan Horse, Duel of the Titans.*"

"He was perhaps better known for his musculature," Kai explains, "than for his thespian ability."

"Having been," Kei continues, "Mr. America, Mr. World and Mr. Universe before moving, in the early 1950s, to Italy, where international stardom awaited him."

Steve whispers into Kei's ear. Kei whispers to Kai, who says to me, "Steve, finding it somewhat warm in your abode, requests kind permission to remove his shirt."

"Be my guest, Steve. It's a running battle Oro and I have about the *kotatsu.*"

Kai nods to Kei who nudges Steve who shucks off his shantung shirt to reveal a torso that, although disproportionate to the rest of his body, being almost as wide as he is tall, is nevertheless impressive in a slablike way.

"Do you think," I say turning to Kai, "we should turn down the *kotatsu* as well?"

"That's entirely up to you, Louise."

"Steve doesn't need hourly basting or anything?"

At last, the merest suggestion of a smile from Kai's sculpted lips. "Steve seeks only to be admired. Other than that, he requires very little maintenance. I, for one, do not find it inordinately warm here."

Oro comes in, face alight, wrapped in a *yukata* I pinched from the Akasaka Pearl. As he moves across the room to welcome his friends, it trails across the tatami like a softly hissing snake.

New introductions are called for, fresh rounds of bowing, followed by shoulder pounding and a big hug for everyone, me included, from Steve, whose bare torso gives off more heat than the red *kotatsu* bulb.

I feel I should slip into my giddy Japanese hostess role, pitch my voice high and sibilant, chatter, giggle and become nauseatingly obsequious, but Oro beats me to it, opening the sake with one hand, tearing the cling wrap off the sushi boxes with the other, meanwhile keeping up a constant welcoming patter. Nagisa—or is it Yasujiro?—offers me a platter of what look like chocolate chip cookies.

"What are these?" I say, taking one.

A huddled conference among Yasujiro—or is it Nagisa?—and Kai and Kei. At last Kai turns to me. "These are Yasujiro's chocolate chip cookies—a very special recipe. Instead of chocolate chips he uses mushrooms. Try not to eat too many, please."

To show what a good sport I am I take one and bite into it. Chewy, just the way I like them, and the mushroom bits are fairly tasteless. I grab a couple more before Yasujiro carries off the platter.

"Uh, Louise," Kai says, trying not to stare at my handful of cookies.

"What?"

"She's a big girl," Oro says and hands Kai two skewers of chicken parts.

Kai bows low in acknowledgment of this self-evident truth and makes like a sword swallower with the chicken parts. Someone hands me a mug of warm sake to wash down the cookies. Over in the corner someone else loads a tape into my VCR: Moira Shearer stands on pointe, red hair sparkling in the key light.

"This is the famous movie *The Red Shoes*," Kai explains. "This is Nagisa's favorite movie. Do you know it?"

Not as well as Nagisa does; he recites *all* the lines along with the actors.

"Has this always been your favorite movie, Nagisa?"

"I am sorry," he bows, "no speak English. 'You can never remove the shoes. You will keep dancing till you die!'"

There is a gap in the party then, as the result of a hole in my consciousness, and when I turn back to the table, the various platters and canisters have been stripped bare, the sake bottles are empty and someone has uncorked both bottles of cognac. One cookie remains on a crumb-speckled plate. I know my hips will regret it in the morning but I can't resist.

At some point Kai slips out of the room and returns carrying an octagonal leather case. He places it on the floor in front of Oro, who claps his hands and says, "Turtle!"

He unzips the case and carefully removes the shining tortoiseshell. After much minute tightening of strings he gives a great rippling strum to call us all to attention. This is not easily accomplished, as Nagisa is doing a frame-by-frame of Moira Shearer's big over-the-balustrade finale and Steve has stripped down to a gold lamé jockstrap, slathered his muscles with baby oil and is pulling poses for Yasujiro and Masahiro in the corner. Oro gives another, sharper strum and everyone freezes. Nagisa mutes the television while Moira continues her articulated leap.

In a graceful speech that freely mixes Japanese and English Oro manages to leave us all bewildered. From what

I gather the song he proposes to sing is either about me or for me. Once he hits the chorus it's clear it's the latter for they all know the song as well as Nagisa knows how to lip-synch *The Red Shoes*. Each verse is plaintive and sad—show me a Japanese ballad that ain't—but the chorus has a slow roll to it. The boys come in at the end of every second line singing, "Toot, toot." The rock and rumble of it is so lulling there are moments I feel I could be anywhere, even back in Lethbridge listening to that lonesome whistle blow. Nostalgic horseshit, since we never lived anywhere near the tracks.

When the song's over, there's no applause, just a long meditative silence. I assume he's going to continue playing—it's his party after all—but instead he puts the tortoiseshell back in its case and smiles to me. "Your turn, Louise."

I shake my head. "No way, baby. Can't sing a note."

"You know one song. Everybody knows one song."

"I know lots of songs, I just don't want to desecrate one by singing it."

He licks his lips. "You sang the other night."

"That wasn't me," I remind him.

"If it wasn't you, who was it?"

"Emptiness."

Everyone laughs.

"There's one song I like, I could *say* it. I learned it from a boy I knew a long time ago. Jean-Louis. He was from Montreal. It's by a French singer named Françoise Hardy:

Et si je m'en vais avant toi   (And if I leave before you do
dis-toi bien que je serai la,   tell yourself I'll be there,

j'épouserai la pluie, le vent,	*I'll marry the rain, the wind,*
le soleil et les éléments	*the sun and the elements*
pour te caresser tout le temps.	*so I can caress you all the time.*
L'air sera tiède et léger,	*The air will be warm and light,*
commes tu aimes.	*the way you like it.*
Et si tu ne comprends pas	*And if you don't understand*
très vite tu me reconnaîtras	*you'll recognize me at once*
car moi je deviendrai méchant.	*for I'll turn nasty.*
J'épouserai une tourmente	*I'll marry a storm*
pour te faire mal et te faire froid.	*to torment you and freeze you.*
L'air sera désespéré comme	*The air will turn as despairing*
ma peine.	*as my pain.*
Et si pourtant tu nous oublies,	*And if nevertheless you forget,*
Il me faudra laisser la pluie,	*I'll be forced to leave the rain,*
le soleil et les éléments	*the sun and the elements*
et je te quitterai vraiment	*and I'll leave you for real*
et nous quitterai aussi.	*and leave us too.*
L'air ne sera que du vent	*The air will be only a wind*
comme l'oubli.	*like forgetfulness.)*

This time there's applause all around because they know that's what *gaijin* like. I put my palms together and give the kind of humility bow you see Mother Theresa performing for television crews at international airports.

"But what does this song mean?" Oro says.

Kai leaps in. "If I understood correctly, the person in the song is telling her beloved that if he forgets her she will—"

"—cut off his balls and have them for breakfast."

Oro gets a big kick out of this, laughing and slapping his knees. Thinks I'm joking. When he recovers he says, "Kai, Kei, it's your turn now. Better be very good."

They leap jointless to their feet, strip off their shirts and fling them aside. Bow to the room at large, to me, to Oro, to everyone else, to each other. Then Kai hauls off and smacks Kei across the face. Kei flies backward through the air, at the last moment reverse-somersaulting into a standing position. He bows once more and swings his left leg round so it clips Kai in the jaw. Kai flips over the table, pikes, rolls and comes up grinning in front of me.

"That's fucking amazing. How'd you do that?"

"Kai and Kei best stuntmen in"—Oro counts on small fingers—"Tokyo, Hong Kong and Taipei. They work on my new samurai movie."

"Please, Louise." Kai holds out his hands and helps me to my feet. "We will show you a few simple tricks."

It's only on the third one, which involves Kai charging my right, Kei my left and me stepping aside at the last moment while twisting their wrists so that they arc gracefully over my shoulders and double-somersault to the floor, that I lose my balance—stepping back is such a complicated move—crash through the shoji screens and land on my back on the veranda. Kai and Kei tumble out after me, followed closely by Oro and the others. As they help me to my feet, a sudden flash of lightning illuminates the veranda, the splintered wood, ripped rice paper.

Oro turns his head, alert, wide-eyed. "Everybody into the house," he cries, "quick-quick."

"It's only a thunderstorm," I try to say but Oro covers my mouth with one hand and they bundle me back inside.

Oro looks into my eyes. "Did you tell people I would be here?"

I shake my head. "Maybe it's one of my students. They're so curious about my—" I make a mental note to throttle Keiko next time I see her.

"Maybe," Oro says. "Maybe not."

"What's wrong?"

"Maybe we have a big problem. Maybe there are journalists in bushes, behind the wall. Disgusting."

"Why would they ...?" I start to say, then remember who he is, see the thousands of fans staring up at us as the Osaka restaurant slowly revolved. Everything he does is of intrinsic interest to millions and millions of people. This strikes me as peculiar. I break into laughter.

Oro looks at me. "Not so funny."

"I know." I stifle my giggles. "Too many cookies."

"May we"—Oro stretches out his arms to include his friends—"stay the night please?"

"Of course." I have two futons and three rose-patterned eiderdowns or whatever they're called here. We use one of the eiderdowns to cover the hole in the shoji screens. Oro turns the kotatsu bulb up so high the whole room glows red. We spread the futons side by side and I lie down in the middle, with Steve, blocky heating unit that he is, on one side and Oro on the other. Kai and Kei bookend them, Nagisa and Masahiro curl at our feet, with Yasujiro's thigh for our pillow.

Once we're all settled in, leather jackets and sweaters piled atop the thin eiderdowns, I start to giggle again.

"What wrong, Louise?" Oro says.

I'm too exhausted to explain about Snow White and her seven little men.

16

Away

A little low today. Fog seeps into the valley, lids the sky. Is this pathetic fallacy or just plain pathetic? Oro and the boys didn't get away till after six, and then only with the most theatrical stealth. Fifteen minutes before departure time, two Land Rovers roared up and down the service road that parallels the compound wall—"securing the corridor," Kai called it. Men with walkie-talkies lurked behind every second fir, but the paparazzi were long gone, leaving behind them only empty film canisters, Mosburger wrappings and dead mickeys of cheap whiskey. By the time the boys got away I decided to skip breakfast and go back to bed—figured I could get in an hour's nap before class.

Class turned out to be a real bomb. Keiko sulked because I wasn't paying her enough attention. Michiko tried to improvise a love song for our show, but Noriko laughed during the first chorus and she burst into tears. I let them go early, which Madame Watanabe no doubt took note of. After lunch—a particularly unctuous fish splayed across a bed of yesterday's rice—I went to the far end of the compound to the Graceful Statement Design Studio to meet with Mrs. Yanagi from wardrobe and Mr. Sasaki, who's second-in-command for sets and properties.

Mrs. Yanagi is plump as a pineapple with copper-colored hair that sprouts from a cunning arrangement of multicolored scarves. Despite the vagueness of my descriptions, she grasps what I'm after.

"Only black and white," she confirms, "no color nobody."

"And lots of chiaroscuro," I add.

"What is?" Her rouged cheeks inflate with concentration.

"Modeling of color and light—not only black and white but all the shades of gray in between. Like an old movie. You know how on film black looks like ebony or onyx, but sometimes it has the texture of charcoal or wool? And white often looks silvery or like ivory, and other times it's chalky or satiny like cold cream."

She nods vigorously, ceramic penguin earrings bobbing. "You want like old Paramount films, 1930s? Or maybe RKO?"

"I was thinking more recent than that. More the way French movies looked in the sixties."

She scribbles in a small spiral notebook and looks up at me. "Very experimental, Louise."

"That's what I'm aiming for."

"Not Heartful Purity house style at all," she suggests with a discreet smile.

"Exactly."

"Nice change," she says. "Many nights I dream pastel nightmares."

The big high-ceilinged workroom where they build the sets is one floor down from Mrs. Yanagi's atelier. At first Mr. Sasaki, in spite of our appointment, is nowhere to be found. White-gloved assistants and aproned apprentices criss-cross the long room calling his name. Once found, crouched sucking tea through saffron-colored teeth behind a forced perspective model of the Taj Mahal, he is still not available. He must sip slowly while the *gaijin* interloper cools her heels. Once available—he hawks and lungers on the concrete floor—he proves intractable.

First, it is impossible to build any set at all, a translator with pigskin gauntlets up to his elbows conveys.

"Why is that, Mr. Sasaki?"

Sasaki-*san* glowers at me and looks as if he may spit again. Instead he gurgles in the assistant's ear.

"No budget for *gaijin* project," the assistant affirms. "No budget code or approval number."

I pull out my big gun. "Arakawa-*san* said I could have whatever I wanted, within reason of course."

It takes the assistant many minutes to explain this to Mr. Sasaki, who responds with a guttural interjection followed by the phrase "Arakawa-*san*."

I can see we're getting somewhere. On an adjacent drafting table I lay out hasty sketches I've made of the sets I need: a modern hotel room with big rectangular plate glass windows, a street scene chaotic with neon signs, the interior of a nightclub called The Oasis.

Mr. Sasaki glances contemptuously at these and with a blunt pencil corrects the vanishing lines on the nightclub drawing, all the time muttering away. I hear a single intelligible word: "Showbusiness."

The assistant turns to me, eyes full of sadness at having to transmit such daunting words. "Sasaki-*san* say your drawings impossible to execute, they are work of five-year-old with no special talent and little sense of theater. No one will want to look at your sets even if he builds them, which cannot be done in any case. And if people do look at them, it will be only in horror, for your sets betray all principles of School of Heartful Purity, they betray traditions and conventions of set design and, finally, they demonstrate once and for all you have no sense of showbusiness."

I bow low to the assistant, lower to Mr. Sasaki. "Please thank Mr. Sasaki for his co-operation and support. I am sure our collaboration will prove a fruitful one."

I leave the resounding workroom before the assistant has finished translating Mr. Sasaki's reply.

—

Head back to my bungalow intending to crawl into bed and stay there at least until suppertime, but Hermiko crouches on my veranda. She glances at the hole in the shoji screens, the rose-patterned eiderdown billowing in the cool breeze. "Quite a party, Louise."

"News travels fast."

"Faster than you think." She holds up a Japanese newspaper. Above the front-page fold is a photograph of me lying on my back, legs in the air, a shirtless Kai and Kei pulling at my arms while in the background Steve gives off a baby-oil sheen. Over to one side Oro, looking wary, stares directly into the camera.

I unfold the paper. In the bottom right-hand corner is a *color* photo of the Princess of Wales in a silly hat. "What is this paper, Hermiko? And why does Princess Di get color and I'm in grainy black-and-white?"

"This is *Starry Jumpo*, Japan's equivalent of the *National Enquirer*. No one admits to buying it but everyone knows what's in every issue. I bought it at the Heartful Purity gift shop."

"Do you think anyone else has seen it?"

"I saw your students fighting over a copy in the Cocoon lounge after lunch. Mr. Arakawa is very concerned."

"He's seen it?"

"That's why I'm here." Hermiko touches my arm and indicates I crouch, or at least sit next to her. "As his unofficial emissary. I am to inspect the damage and tactfully suggest you refrain from entertaining your famous friend and his boisterous chums within the Heartful Purity Compound."

"Oh God, Hermiko, I feel like such an idiot. It wasn't supposed to be a party. I invited Oro and he—"

"—brought along the usual camp followers. I know how he is, but you can understand Mr. Arakawa's position?"

"Of course I do."

She looks into my eyes. "You must be very careful, you know. For your own sake as well as the school's. Oro is a lightning rod. The tabloid press are constantly trying to catch him out. The time has come for him to marry—he's almost thirty you know—and yet he has not married, has even spoken of marriage with some disdain in interviews. This has caused great curiosity to arise among journalists and his millions of fans. As well as many unusual rumors."

Almost thirty? "I thought he was James Dean—he can do whatever he likes."

"He can do anything he wants as long as he doesn't get caught."

"I see." I study my legs-in-the-air image once more. "Does this count as getting caught?"

"Oro is supposed to avoid being romantically linked with anyone specific. His managers claim it hurts box office. At the same time, to dispel awkward rumors he must go on very public dates with a variety of stars and starlets. And even when he chooses to see someone seriously, he likes to think he can keep that part of his life private."

"Good luck. Can you tell me what it says under the picture?"

She studies the caption for a moment. "You're sure you want to know? Let's see: 'Riotous party at mountain villa of *gaijin* mystery woman finds superstar Oro taken by surprise. Pinning the large woman to the ground for Oro's pleasure are the renowned stuntmen Kai and Kei Fujimori.'"

"Fuck, Hermiko. Can Heartful Purity break my contract over this?"

"You have no contract here. You know that. Everything's done on a handshake, or rather a bow."

"Was Mr. Arakawa furious?"

"More bemused than anything else. He had you down as 'a nice quiet girl.'"

"Should I start packing?"

"I don't think that will be necessary. As a foreigner you're allowed a certain leeway. Foreigners are expected to fuck up—it's seen as part of your colorful alien charm."

"That's a relief."

Hermiko grins. "So I guess you must have had a pretty good time?"

"From what I can remember."

"I've contacted Compound Services to come and repair your shoji screens."

"Thanks. You want to come in for some tea or something? The place is a complete mess."

"Sure."

The futons are still spread on the floor, eiderdowns trail across the tatami.

"Goodness," Hermiko says, "did you sleep with all of them?"

"After a fashion." I switch on the electric kettle and start clearing party debris from the table.

Hermiko discovers a half-full bottle of cognac on top of the VCR. "Forget the tea."

I pour us each a generous tumbler and we recline on the futons. Hermiko reaches out and brushes a clump of curls back off my forehead. "Why so glum, Louise?"

"I don't know. I ..."

"You're not to take Mr. Arakawa's reprimand too much to heart. In a week all this will have blown over. And you can continue seeing Oro, only at his place." She laughs. "Or you could always go to a love hotel."

—

The phone rings in the middle of the night.

"Oro?"

"How did you know?"

"Who else would call at this hour?"

"Sorry."

"No you're not. You basically don't give a fuck."

He chuckles. "What are you doing tomorrow?"

"What's it to you?"

"You are very angry?" The tone of his voice suggests he'd enjoy nothing better.

"Oro, you got me in a lot of trouble."

"The picture in the newspaper?"

"Among other things."

He laughs. "Good picture."

"Of you. I look like the whore of Babylon."

"Legs in the air. Dirty crazy girl."

"Well, it can't happen again."

"Never?"

"At least not at my place. I could lose my job."

"Oh. This is very serious. I am sorry."

Funny how I can feel him bow. "So what's happening tomorrow?"

"A surprise."

I don't think I could survive another one. "Is it going to be just you or you and the boys?"

"Just me."

"Kyoto?"

"Tokyo. A car comes for you one o'clock. This is all right?"

"This is all right."

"I will see you tomorrow evening." The line crackles.

"Oro, where are you?"

"No place."

"Where?"

"On a beach."

"Isn't it freezing?"

"A beach in Fiji."

"Never mind. I'm going back to sleep. I'm a working girl."

"Me too." He giggles. "See you tomorrow, large *gaijin* mystery woman."

"Oro?"

"Yes, Louise?"

"Go fuck yourself."

—

The Maserati speeds along a wide tree-lined boulevard in a part of Tokyo I haven't seen before. I lean forward and call to the driver, "Where are we?"

"Between Harajuku and Shibuya," he says and goes back to sucking his gums.

Make a note of that. Fashionable area. About a million girls with seventeen-inch waists carrying Hanae Mori shopping bags.

We curve past a big leafy park and an enormous poured-concrete ark. "Yoyogi Stadium," the driver calls back to me. "Tokyo Olympic."

"Are we nearly there?"

He brakes hard and turns around to grin at me. "There."

A long plaza that ends in a big blocky modern building. The sign says NHK Hall. The plaza's deserted. Just then the sun sets the way it does in Japan, like someone switching off the lights.

"You sure this is right?" I say to the driver.

He pushes a button on the dash and my door swings open. I get out and adjust the veil on my hat—Hermiko's idea, as are the plum-colored cocktail dress and the black brocade jacket. Normally I try not to wear anything from the violet end of the spectrum, but most of my hair is tucked up under the hat, and the veil—"for security purposes," according to Hermiko—covers any stray tendrils.

I'm halfway to the main door when he scuttles up. Incognito in dark glasses and a suit sharp as a shark's fin.

"I would never have recognized you, small Japanese movie star."

"Nice hat, Louise. Nice ... what do you call this?" He passes a hand across his eyes.

"Veil."

"Veil—that's right," he repeats. "I would like one for me too. Good idea."

"Usually they're for women, but I don't see why you shouldn't."

"Did you have nice flight?"

"A bit bumpy." In a small silver chopper instead of the big black one.

"I am so sorry."

"And the Maserati, Oro. Midnight blue is such a tired color, don't you think?"

"Really?"

I start to laugh. "I'm pulling your leg." He looks down at his legs to see which one. "I'm teasing."

He nods. "I don't get it."

"Never mind."

"We must hurry-hurry." He takes my arms and speeds me along the plaza.

"We're going to a concert?"

"Rehearsal," he says.

A dozen men in navy suits materialize behind the lobby's glazed doors. Much mimed embarrassment follows: none of them thought to bring the key.

At last we are inside, cruising along subterranean corridors behind the suits. They halt at a mat black double door. The doors open, music pours out. The suits stand aside and Oro and I walk in. A room the size of a high school gym, with a full orchestra crammed against the far wall and a chorus of hundreds on risers, their backs to us.

We sidle along the periphery of the room, past bowing factotums, stepping over open plush-lined instrument cases that dangle tags reading OSM/MSO JAPAN TOUR. We find a couple of folding chairs set up next to the violas, already darkly sawing away. As we sit down the chorus comes in, nearly knocking us over. We turn to look, I snag the sleeve of my jacket on an empty music stand. It angles toward the floor in a flash of silver. An instant before it hits the parquet I catch it with one finger. Look up, smiling apologetically—I would bow if I weren't already nearly prostrate—into a wall of tubby pasty-faced zombies, all of them with their mouths open, chewing away as though they're in the middle of devouring the back row of the boys' choir spread out in front of them. Only then does it hit me that the first three rows of the massive choir are perfectly formed little Japanese boys in neat black tunics, faces aglow and quivering like candle flames in the room's murky light. The rows and rows of adult singers ranged behind them are all *gaijins*, not chewing but madly singing, their big *bouches* flapping open and shut. The conductor, a balding guy in a blue nylon windbreaker, cuts them off mid-chew and elegantly hectors them in a mixture of French and English.

"Oro," I whisper, "what is this?"

"Montreal Orchestra Symphony. Japan Tour," he beams.

Canadians! No wonder they look so awful. OK, so this is only a rehearsal, but why are some of them seated, some standing and all of them badly dressed? Oh, let's be fair: overdressed. The room is warm and close, yet they're all layered as though awaiting Peary's command to trudge north. Men with tweed jackets draped over cardigans buttoned over turtlenecks. Women in designer sweaters large enough to house your average Japanese family. And their skin! Whoever first thought to call this race white? They are gray as newsprint, dun as toast, sallow as tallow—not one is close to any shade of white. Some of the younger ones have pink cheeks, a few of the older ones have red noses from drink or colds. Holy smoke but they're a grim lot. Pot-bellied, bandy-legged, sway-backed, graceless, formless—nothing for it but to cart them off to the knacker's.

The bald guy taps his baton on the podium. "*Numéro soixante-cinq, s'il vous plaît.* Remember, *legato.*"

A tracery of oboes, the French horns chrome in. Three ladies in late middle age—they've been sitting on folding chairs in the first row of the adult chorus—decide they'll stand up for this bit and do so with the maximum amount of clatter, fabric smoothing and hair patting. I *know* these ladies, with their long pleated skirts and creaking leather boots, their bad perms and designer spectacles with lenses the size of windshields. Before their cue one of them abruptly sits down again and, as the boys' choir flutes on, rummages in her purse and produces a plastic inhaler. Jet lag, or the terrible Tokyo pollution, or stress, or all three, has made her asthma act up. She inserts the nozzle in her mouth, has one puff, then another. Much better. She's back on her feet just in time to sing.

I am unprepared. Rich adult voices swell the room. My ladies are not beautiful—but they are part of beauty now, which is more than I ever figured them for. Of course I can't hear each one of them singing. They may be flat or sharp or, too heavy on the vibrato, bleating like sheep. Nevertheless they are part of the wave that rushes toward and washes over Oro and me, and when their time is over my ladies look pale and spent, startled even, as if they know only the music saves them from themselves. This effort of *sauvetage* becomes more immense with every note sung. It involves pulling buckets up from an inner well and spilling them out toward us to make the wave. There is no replenishment, only depletion. Even as they sing do they sense that one day the bucket will rise up dry as bone? Morning beauty turns to evening bones, the world is changing without end. They sing on anyway, a kind of courage.

The conductor breaks in once more, dissatisfied.

"I know this is Mahler," I murmur to Oro, "but which one?"

He reaches into the breast pocket of his suit to produce a silver-faced notebook with a tiny mechanical pencil dangling from a chain. Opening it he reads: "Symphony Number Eight, also known as *Symphony of a Thousand*, by Gustav

Mahler, written in six weeks in 1906. 'Imagine that the universe bursts into song. We hear no longer human voices, but those of planets and suns which revolve.'"

"Where'd you get that, Oro?"

"The notebook? In Venice two years ago."

"No, the stuff about the symphony."

"One of my assistants."

"Anything else?"

He consults the notebook. "After they will play 'Kindertotenlieder,' 'The Dead Children Song.' For orchestra and one singer only. 'Song laments not only children dying young—Mahler's brothers, his daughter—but also the loss of an innocent view of life.'"

"Can we stay for that? It's one of my all-time favorites."

He touches my hand just as the orchestra strikes up again. "We will stay for the whole thing, Louise. A present from Canada for you."

—

The twelve suits let us out of NHK Hall. The long plaza's empty, lamps on curving poles cast ovals of light at regular intervals. Then it's not empty. Three guys with video cameras on their shoulders charge out of the shrubbery that edges the plaza and scramble toward us full tilt, switching on floodlights as they run. Then another thirty or forty men and women stampede across the plaza. Some carry cameras with powerful flashes, others hold out silver microphones.

I pull the tassel on the side of my hat and the veil rings down like a little stage curtain. I can see them but they can't see me—the world's grainy as an old movie. I feel strangely calm, unreachable.

Oro glances over at me, takes my hand. "Don't be afraid, please," he says, then registers the veil. He smiles. "Very good. Do not run. We will walk, very calm. Heads up, eyes open."

A few more steps and they're on us like a miasma. I can smell what the closest ones had for dinner, or had instead of dinner. "Oro, Oro," they shout, followed by questions I don't understand. My feet leave the ground and he and I are borne along.

A sharp-faced woman in a yellow jacket comes right up to the veil and breathes into it. The humidity of her mouth leaves a dark circle on the translucent fabric just below my nose. "Louise," she says. "This is your name, is it not?"

I go as blank as possible, the skin on my face a second veil.

"You talk to me, Louise." She tries to slip the silver tube of her microphone under the veil. "Tell me how you got Oro, tell my listeners what you do to captivate Japan's movie star number one."

We're carried forward, the cameramen run backwards in front of us.

"Louise, Louise," she purrs. "Please tell us your secrets of love. Everyone in Japan want to know ..." A guy with a hand-held video camera knocks her out of the way but she's back in an instant, one hand tugging at the lapel of my jacket. "Everyone in Japan have to know, Louise, how a big *gaijin* such as yourself can cast a spell on Japan's James Dean."

I can see the Maserati in the distance. The back door swings open automatically.

She's starting to get on my nerves. I try to take my cue from Oro, who moves along as though hypnotized. They are all over him but he is not there.

"Show us your face, Louise. Show us your ugly *gaijin* face." She grabs at the veil and pulls.

I give her—oh, just a little poke in the solar plexus. She's small, though, lightweight, maybe I ought to have factored that in. She reels backwards over a guy in a safari jacket who has crouched down to get a better angle on my humongous tits. She's down on the concrete. And out.

My veil hangs by a thread. Flash. Flash. Flash. I want to wait and see if blood slowly seeps out from under her head the way it does in movies, but Oro's got me by one arm, his driver has the other and they transport me across the remaining twenty yards to the car as the mob swarms around us.

The door slams, we re-pave the street with high-grade Michelin rubber.

Oro's face is right up against mine. "What did you do, Louise? What did you do?"

"I clocked her one."

"Clock?"

The driver looks over his shoulder, laughing.

"I gave her a little push."

Oro's brow furrows. "Very bad. Oh, this is very bad, Louise." He pounds my shoulder. "The new Muhammad Ali."

"Ali Muhammad," the driver chortles.

—

When I finally get up the newspapers are spread across the long brushed-steel workbench that serves as Oro's dining table. The layout's the same in almost all of them. On the

left a grainy enlargement of my startled face from the black-
and-white photo of me sprawled on my veranda at Heartful
Purity. In the middle a color close-up of me, veil askew so
that one eye shows, glaring like a cornered animal's. My
lipstick's smudged, red curls poke madly out from under my
hat. On the right a photo of a heavily bandaged head with
an IV drip hanging beside it.

Oro comes around the floor-to-ceiling aquarium that's
full of darting lemon carp and about three cubic feet of
aquamarine glass marbles. He wears a short white silk dressing gown and carries an espresso pot.

"Good morning, Louise."

I point to the red ink headline that runs over the photos
in one of the splashier-looking papers. "What's it say?"

He stares at it for a moment. "It says, 'Who Is Lady of
Evening Faces?'"

"Is that a subtle Japanese way of calling me a whore?"

"It comes from an old book."

I bet. "What's it say underneath?"

"Lots of things. It's not important. You want coffee?"

I nod. "What things?"

"Stupid things. Disgusting."

"What?"

"About who you are. What you do." He pauses. "How
you look."

"Translate it, please."

"Louise, this is very disgusting stuff. I don't—"

"Shut up and translate."

"This writer says you are like an ugly witch with big
mouth and teeth like mah-jong tiles. She says, Oro waits so

long to fall in love and now this. He rejects all Japanese woman for a *gaijin* woman and she is not even a pretty *gaijin* woman—no blonde hair, for example. This is an insult to all Japanese woman. She is big and fat, this *gaijin* woman— twice, maybe three times the size of our Oro, Japanese movie star number one."

"Thank you."

He pushes the cup of espresso toward me. "They say these things because they are angry. You are not fat or ugly. *Gaijin*, yes. Big, yes. I like big, I like the foreign barbarian. Not like little skinny Japanese. You are different, Louise. Everybody in Japan is the same. I am different too. This is why I love."

He hasn't said that word before. I won't say it at all. "And my big ugly Western mouth, my huge teeth—what do you think about them?"

"Very beautiful, very different. I love ..." He stops, pours himself more espresso, knocks it back. "I love them. I love you, Louise."

"No, you don't."

He looks up, startled. "No? I have never loved anyone before. I think it could never happen to me. Now you tell me I do not love you. You are saying you do not love me?"

"You like being with me, I like being with you. It's fun. Exciting. Good sex."

"Good sex," he nods and flips up the back of his short dressing gown to refresh my memory of his cheeks.

"And you have a very nice butt."

"Number one in Japan."

"But love is like being held prisoner in a bad play: you've got to say the same lines every night, night after night, or the whole thing collapses. I want you, Oro, I just don't want anything more than that, OK?"

He turns away and walks the length of his flat, which takes some time. The place is one enormous room. It looks like a parking garage, the concrete floor painted a dirty gold, the furniture, what there is of it, brushed steel. A series of tall sliding-glass doors give onto a terrace that surrounds the flat, but the terrace is so wide and we're up so high that from inside all you can see are the motionless gray clouds of the Tokyo sky.

When he comes back he says, "OK," and disappears behind the aquarium once more.

The phone rings. He talks a long time. He's naked when he comes in again, hard dick preceding him by about four inches. The scar that bisects his torso glows amber.

"Journalist you clock in coma. We must go away right away. Not right away. First I fuck you, but no love, OK?"

"Got it."

—

The black helicopter sets us down on a deserted pier that juts out into Kobe harbor. As he climbs down Oro points out a low-slung boat the same dark blue as his Maseratis. "Hydrofoil," he says. "The helicopter scares the monkeys."

Right. Behind us Kobe sprawls across a range of steep hills, a sleepy provincial city as different from Kyoto as Kyoto is from Tokyo. It would be nice to take an hour or two to stroll about, visit the tourist sites, stop someplace for coffee or a beer. For Oro, though, for me with Oro, none of these is an option. Ordinary is out of the question now, and I kind of miss it. It occurs to me that Oro may never have known it to begin with.

A young man in a gold-buttoned white jacket helps me up the gangway. Oro follows. As we're about to cast off a girl on a gold motor scooter comes putting along the pier. She pulls up at the foot of the gangway, bows to the boat and unstraps a small red leather suitcase from the scooter's carrier rack.

"Who's that?" I ask Oro as the suitcase is brought on board.

"An assistant," he says.

"What's her name?"

"Assistant. How would I know? She works for me, lives in Kobe. The suitcase is for you."

"For me?"

"All the things you need for an island weekend."

A lot of the time it feels like he's not there, that he sails above the rest of us, detachment and self-containment complete. Maybe the perspective's better up there: he doesn't miss much. It hits me that what I like most about Oro is that he is untouchable but not remote—from me at least.

Another white-jacketed young man holds open the cabin door. Strips of dark-tinted windows run along either side of the cabin, which is fitted with long black leather sofas. In the center of the room stands a fancy sandbox, a rectangle rimmed in black marble and full of fine gray sand that has been raked and molded to form the outline of a perfect square: □. "Mouth," I remember, my single Japanese character. Exit. Way Out. Handy in a subway or a conflagration.

On the other side of the sandbox, a group of older men in suits surround a middle-aged woman in a frantically ruffled silk dress swirled with gold and umber leaves. Gold foil leaves and a scattering of gold coins have been woven into her abundant black hair. She catches my eye—an unusual thing for a Japanese woman to do—and smiles. One of the suited men turns around: Mr. Arakawa from Heartful Purity.

"Oro," I whisper, "what is this? I thought we were going away alone."

"We will be alone. But I have a business meeting first." He takes my hand. "Louise, already you know Mr. Arakawa, head of Heartful Purity School. Please meet Mr. Kobayashi, director of Idée-Fixe Department Store Chain, and Mr. Shinoda, CEO of Komori Toy and Entertainment Enterprises, Mr. Naruse, president of Hurry-Curry Fastfood, and Mr. Anaka, who runs Komakai Investments. And this is Mrs. Anaka ..."

Camille Anaka, RN, steps forward, clasps me to her lopsided bosom and surreptitiously kneads my bum. "Louise, long time no saw. When you come for bath again?" She turns to her husband, a tiny man with a shining brown pate and a mustache that's little more than silver down. "Louise teach me English in Kyoto. Very good teacher. With Louise we laugh and learn."

Mr. Arakawa comes over to take my hand. "Louise teach our Heartful Purity girls more than English. She teach life."

Much bowing and laughter in acknowledgment of my

promiscuous talent. So jovial I almost forget to smell the rat.
There follows one of those long-drawn-out pauses that the
Japanese affect to find perfectly normal, even soothing, and
that make me crazy. Each time one occurs I steel myself not
to be the first to speak, but then, inevitably, I am.

"So how do you all know Oro?" I say.

Much general laughter that translates as, "Isn't the *gaijin*
cute but indelicate?"

Mr. Arakawa leads me over to a long stretch of sofa.
"Louise, you know Oro as talented singer, Japan movie star
number one, perhaps you know *Maku Hama* television series
also. He ..."

Mr. Anaka breaks in. "Oro entertainer, big showbiz guy,
but also big business. Our business"—he nods toward Mr.
Arakawa, Mr. Kobayashi, Mr. Shinoda and Mr. Naruse—
"because together we make up Shiru Entertainment Conglomerate."

Mrs. Anaka beams at me. "Most important showbiz conglomerate in Japan."

"In Asia," her husband corrects her.

"What does *shiru* mean?" I say to Oro.

He stares at the ceiling. "Brown stuff you put on rice."

"Sauce," Mr. Anaka says.

"Gravy," Mrs. Anaka adds.

The hydrofoil's up on its sea legs, planing along. Small
rocky islands flash past. The Inland Sea looks more like a
wide channel than a real sea, the water beyond the boat's
wake a tranquil tarnished gray.

"We don't want to disturb your holiday with Oro," Mr.
Kobayashi says. "He work hard, deserve rest, but important

we have conference for ... for ..." He struggles to find a tactful way of putting it in English.

"Damage control?" I supply.

Sage nods all around. "Scandal good," Mr. Naruse volunteers, smiling and licking his lips. "Up to point."

"Good when we control publicity," Mr. Shinoda says. "When publicity control us, then trouble."

Oro has been sitting quietly, hands clasped under his chin, watching them, watching me. "What happened was not Louise's fault. The lady journalist tripped, fell down."

"No one say," Mr. Anaka says, "Louise problem. Lady journalist bad fruit. Always make troubles."

"Good riddance," Mrs. Anaka sniffs.

"We have video that prove," Mr. Anaka continues, "she not in coma. Newspaper put her in private rest home to keep story alive. Nothing wrong with head but big bump. Put on bandages for photos."

"They do anything for story," Mr. Shinoda confirms. "Lie, cheat, steal, pay money."

"So if the lady journalist's not the problem, and I'm not the problem, exactly what is the problem?" When in doubt my role here is to blunder in wielding a blunt instrument.

"Problem is," Mr. Kobayashi says, putting his fingertips together, "public perception."

"Perception?" Mrs. Anaka murmurs to her husband.

"We have reason to believe," Mr. Kobayashi says, "that a large part of Oro's public resent his association with"—he pauses to take a deep breath—"a foreigner. You all remember three years ago when Oro was romantically involved with that starlet ... what was her name?"

"Tuesday Harada," Mr. Shinoda growls.

"Tuesday Harada?" I can't help repeating.

"Tuesday is half-Japanese, half-American," Mr. Kobayashi explains. "Blue eyes but Japanese features. Even there we found a strong sense of betrayal among Oro's female fans, and Tuesday is half-Japanese, she speaks Japanese fluently and she's very beautiful."

Three strikes I'm out. "So what are my choices, deportation or radical cosmetic surgery?"

No one laughs except Oro and he stops pretty quick at a look from Mr. Anaka.

Mr. Arakawa leans forward, hands on knees. "We are here to help. Part of weekend is for considering this problem. We like you 100 percent, Louise. But we need to find a solution so that you and Oro can be together *and* his career can go on like before."

When a big orderly homogeneous society starts talking solutions, is it paranoid to feel paranoid?

The hydrofoil arcs into a wide harbor. "We arrive," Oro announces and stands. Everyone else gets up as well. A sudden jolt plops Mrs. Anaka back in her seat, gold coins in her hair jingling.

"Hang on, Mrs. Anaka," I say, "it's going to be a bumpy ride."

—

Our truncated motorcade—a Bentley for the Shiru Conglomerate directors, a vintage Jaguar XKE for Oro and me and an Alfa-Romeo station wagon for the staff and provisions—ferries us inland along a road that winds through low scrubby hills. We pass a grove of fan-branched trees

with small silvery leaves that catch the light. "Are those
olive trees?" I ask Oro.

He glances out the window and nods.

"I didn't know they had olive trees in Japan."

"Only here. Shodoshima means 'Olive Island.'"

"Olive trees are native to Japan?"

"What you mean, 'native'?"

"They've always been here?"

He shakes his head. "Brought from Greece a long time
ago."

The terrain grows rougher, drier. We pass through a narrow gap in a rank of reddish perpendicular rocks that loom
like sentinels over a shallow valley. The Bentley turns onto
a gravel road which ends abruptly at a wooden palisade. A
buzzer sounds and the high gates swing open. Olive groves
line both sides of the drive. Their leaves shimmer and whisper in the breeze. It smells of salt and dry earth. The house
is long and low, like a hacienda, with a roof of shiny blue
tiles. A veranda runs the length of it, translucent sliding
screens at regular intervals under the eaves.

"This is where I was born." He pulls the Jag up next to
the Bentley. The station wagon tools around to the back of
the house.

"It's very beautiful. Very plain."

"My mother designed it. A traditional Japanese villa."

"Your mother's an architect?"

"My mother was a big Japanese singer in the sixties,
movie star too. Dead now."

"Was your father in show business too?"

He looks away. "My father is dead as well."

"I'm sorry." I don't mean to bow but I do.

"I am not," he says with a slight smile. He touches his chest. "He gave me this scar. He was also founder of Shiru Entertainment Conglomerate."

Mrs. Anaka and the others step out of the Bentley. "Lovely, lovely," she exclaims and claps her hands.

Oro bows to her and ushers us into the house.

—

He spends most of the afternoon in a conference that doesn't include me. For a while I stay in our room at the far end of the house, trying to read Ross Macdonald's *Trouble Follows Me.* His terseness makes me edgier. The shoji screens are open about six inches so I get a thin slice of garden. I push them all the way back so the fourth wall disappears, slide open the screens at the opposite end of the room. They give on to a wide expanse of sand raked to suggest a languid and curving art nouveau sea. I think I prefer the garden, which has an irregularly shaped carp pool overhung by ornamental trees, a curving wooden footbridge and at the pond's far edge a cluster of upright terra cotta–colored stones that resemble a frozen waterfall. I try to get into it, let the calm soak into me, but all I can think of is what the men in suits are saying to Oro about me three or four rooms along the veranda.

At last I slip around to the front of the house. Oro's left the keys in the ignition. So what if I don't have a Japanese driver's license? A *gaijin* has poetic license. Spray a little gravel onto the veranda getting the hang of the clutch. Maybe they can rake it into an artful pattern. Heavy clouds are moving in from the east. The road's deserted. I open her up and we leap along until I sail over a rise and nearly plow into the back of a big maroon tour bus. At a twisted tree growing out of a rock the bus turns toward the sea. It pulls into a small parking area and I park next to it.

A young woman in a navy suit alights carrying a small green pennant. Around her waist is slung a heavy leather belt with a battery pack dangling from it. In one hand she holds a microphone, a spiral flex connects it to the battery pack. Three hundred middle-aged Japanese women—OK, maybe fifty—swarm off the bus, all of them in identical green sun visors. They stream up the hill after the guide. Some of them walk backwards to get a better gander at the big-boned *gaijin* gal who follows at a discreet distance. The guide leads them among great slabs of gray and purple stone as she speaks into the microphone. I can make out two words: "Hideyoshi" and "Osaka."

The Japanese ladies scamper over the great stones, squealing their delight. At last I find a small sign in English:

Rocks Left Unshipped to Osaka Castle
In 1583 the great overlord and uniter of Japan Hideyoshi
Toyotomi had about 30,000 men build Osaka Castle.
At this time many granite rocks were shipped from
Shodoshima. These rocks, which were left behind, are
called ZANSEKI: "rocks left over" or ZANNEN ISHI:
"rocks which were sorry not to be in time for shipment."

The rocks that weren't used to construct the castle that I kept glimpsing when Hermiko took me to Osaka for Oro's concert, a long time ago.

The tour guide marches past me, pennant cracking in the wind. "Goodbye," she cries through the microphone. "*Sayonara.*"

"Goodbye," the sun-visored ladies call one by one as they disappear into the bus. "*Sayonara. Sayonara. Sayonara.*"

The air cools and darkens. I stretch out on one of the great slabs, still warm with stored sunlight. For a long time I watch the clouds race to meet the sea, wondering whether the rock I lie on is a ZANSEKI or a ZANNEN ISHI.

A car door slams. Oro stands alone in the parking lot next to the station wagon.

"What are you doing, Louise?"

"I'm seeing the sights. These are the stones that didn't make the cut for—"

"I know. I was born here. I have seen these boring stones many times. Everybody was worried—you disappeared."

"What was I supposed to do, stay in my room and listen to the tatami crackle while you and the board of directors decide how to get rid of me?"

He crosses his arms over his chest. "That's not what we talked about. We were planning my spring tour, new CD launch, two feature films."

"Not a word about me?"

He shakes his head then says, "Maybe one little word."

"And what word might that be?"

"'Discreet.' They want us be careful, Louise. Anaka-*san* says you are 'too impulsive.' I say you are not, then you take my car, drive away. How does this look?"

"I'm sorry, Oro. I was feeling a little restless."

"Business is over for now. I sent them to Twenty-Four Eyes Movie Village, then for dinner at Poetic Monument to Shungetsu Ikuta. They will come back very late."

"Good. So what do we do now?"

"I want to show you something." He opens the passenger door of the station wagon. "Get in."

I open the Jag door. "You get in."

He laughs. "Yes sir."

We whip along the narrow curving road. He says, "You're a good driver. A little fast."

"I taught myself how to drive on the back roads of Alberta. You could go for days without meeting another car."

"Shodoshima is pretty quiet in autumn. Not so many tourists or"—he puts his hands together as though in prayer —"how do you call religious tourists?"

"Double-assholes?"

"I'm serious."

"Pilgrims? A lot of pilgrims come here?"

"In spring. Visit eighty-eight shrines and temples."

"Is that where we're going?"

He pulls a face. "To a temple? Disgusting. We're going to my favorite place."

—

It's like a dilapidated petting zoo, except there's no enclosure to speak of and only a few cages of rusted chain-link. Most are empty although a few contain rarer breeds. One huddled pair have luxuriant black fur striped with white like skunks and a strange staring plump one with black rings around its eyes resembles Simone de Beauvoir. But most of the monkeys—from where I stand I can see hundreds of them—at Wild Monkey Zoo do just what they're supposed to: run wild. Shy mothers rustle in the bushes, their babies scrabble in the dirt. It's their older brothers and fathers you have to watch out for. Silver-furred and big as standard poodles they stalk about sneering and growling low in their throats. Their startling vermilion scrotal sacs swing like pendulums. They back away when I walk toward them. When I turn away they follow so close I can hear them breathe.

Oro they greet like a long-lost friend. Maybe he is. They trail after him everywhere, take hold of his hands and swing them, climb up his thighs and throw spindly arms round his neck.

We head up the mountain behind the zoo. Oro's got a monkey on one shoulder and holds two more by the hand. Another twenty or thirty chatter along behind us. Mothers and babies pop up out of the bushes along the way to survey our progress. I try to make friends with the big guy who leads the cohort at my heels but whenever I turn to make eye contact he ducks or looks away. Why does it surprise me that in Japan even the monkeys are Japanese?

The path narrows and the climb steepens. We pass a plot of bare earth enclosed by a low stone border. A half-dozen small stone figures sprout from the earth. Peering closer I see they're fat stone penises clad in doll clothes—gingham skirts or aprons, little ruffled bonnets. A shriveled orange rests against the base of one of them.

The hair on my arms and the back of my neck stands on end. "What are these?"

Oro looks back over his shoulder. "Dead baby shrine."

"Dead babies are buried here?"

"Maybe not." He considers a moment. "A shrine to Japanese ladies' *abortions*. No dead babies."

Blue mist slides over us. Breaks in the scrubby forest give glimpses of the gray sea. Inside a picket fence near the summit stands a dollhouse-sized pink temple with a smiling stone Buddha in the doorway. The odd thing about the temple is that just outside the fence a large deciduous tree, struck close to the ground by lightning, has crashed through the gateway, withered leaves at Buddha's toes. Instead of clearing away the trunk, whoever maintains the temple has capped both gateway and trunk with a delicate wooden arch, so now the dead tree has become part of the temple, like Kafka's hyenas who invade the holy place so often their invasion becomes part of the ritual.

"I like this temple," I say to Oro as I duck under the arch and clamber over the rough lichen-covered trunk. "It feels right to me—the tree destroyed almost at the root and in its destruction it becomes a part of something else."

Oro stands at the edge of the precipice, staring out. "Nice view," he says.

I light a stick of incense and leave a 500-yen coin in the Twining's Gunpowder Green Tea tin on the altar. Stepping back over the tree trunk and bending under the arch I join Oro at the edge. Everything is layered: blue mist hangs in veils in the air, the slowly churning purple clouds, the gray and serried Inland Sea, the low blue mountains of Honshu beyond.

"Oro ..."

"My father ..."

And now the earth is Jell-O beneath our feet. It waves and rolls, scrolls out from under us. The leader of my cohort loses his shyness and leaps aboard, encircles my pelvis with furry silver arms.

"Oro, what ...?"

A grinding from the mountaintop. A gray boulder the size of a van dislodges and begins a slow roll in our direction. Smaller rocks and scree pound down like hard rain. A line of fir trees on the ridge above us shimmies and, cracking, plummets. A mother with a baby on her back clings to my ankle.

I feel calm. Floating. There are worse places to die.

Oro opens his mouth and sings: *"Bleu, bleu, l'amour est bleu ..."*

A kitschy French song from my adolescence. I look at him as the earth waves us up and down. "How do you know that?"

"One of my mother's big hits."

The boulder bounces off the ledge above us and thuds to the ground a few feet in front of us. Although the earth still buckles and rolls, the boulder stays put. Rocks and pebbles spin past us over the edge.

The earth is still and larger beneath our feet than it has ever felt before.

"Nice earthquake," Oro says as the monkeys climb down off him. "Not so strong."

"Nice song," I answer. My guy doesn't seem to want to let go. He bares white teeth as I pry his left hand from where it oughtn't to be.

—

After dinner Oro leads me along a covered walkway that runs from the main house to a small windowless wooden pavilion. We must look so Japanese, hurrying along the whistling boards in the moonlight in our white *yukata*, which are printed all over with dark blue squares. Inside it's plain style: cedar tongue-and-groove walls and slanted ceiling, a pegged floor, a bench that runs along one wall and, in the center of the room, a wooden barrel almost as tall as me with steps running up to it. Steam rises toward the ceiling. Someone has placed a tray with a ceramic flagon and two lacquer saucers on the top step.

Oro takes a small burnished box from inside his robe. He opens it and lays out on the bench a glass tube of silver liquid and the cleanest set of works I've ever seen outside a doctor's office.

"We're not going to shoot?" I say.

"Not in the vein," Oro says. "In the muscle. Safe but good. The best way with Emptiness. Go right in."

"I don't know, Oro. I'm not a junkie."

"I am not either. It's easy. You know how you take vitamin injections?"

I shake my head. "My vitamins come in pills."

"It OK. I don't want to make you nervous."

It's weird. With the aptly named Peter I never once had the urge to share a bit of brown with him. That was his gig, I was there for the sideshow. Now I think, even if Oro asked me to mainline with him, it wouldn't be a problem. The point is to be with him whatever the weather. And he isn't asking *that*. Intramuscularly is child's play, if your child happens to be, say, diabetic. God bless the child that's got his own.

Finally I say, "Emptiness is all," and bare my thigh.

He inserts the needle in the end of the tube and watches the glass cylinder fill with silver. With the nail of his index finger he clicks the glass, squirts a few drops into the air and eases the needle into my flesh. I can feel it stream into me, quake along under my skin.

Sometime later he points at the front of my *yukata*. I look down. Moist circles grow over both my breasts.

He undoes the sash, opens my robe. The viscous liquid trickles from my nipples, clear as tears.

He licks the left one. "Milk," he says and returns to suck. "Delicious," he says a few minutes later before moving on to its round twin.

When there's no more to be had he wipes his mouth and grins. Picking up the syringe he injects the rest of the Emptiness into his leg. "Oh, it is good," he says, slapping his thigh.

Untying the sash he removes his robe. My turn to suck. He tastes like the sea.

"We go into the bath?" he says.

"Not if it's going to scald my skin off."

He pushes the robe off my shoulders, it crumples to the floor. I follow him up the short flight of stairs. "You will be all right," he says and presses a button on a panel set into the side of the barrel. The ceiling splits and rolls back to reveal a long cloud about to pierce the full moon. "Look." He points to the water's clear steaming surface. "You can see the moon."

All I see is his face, reflected in the water, backlit by the moon.

"What do you feel?"

Old joke now. "Nothing."

"Slide in quick as an eel."

With the roof open what it feels like is stepping out into the stillness of the hottest summer night—overwhelmed as you're enveloped. Too hot to stay, too late to move.

He is beside me, inside me, head between my breasts under the water's surface. I suckle him, thinking he should be coming up for air soon. Except, it dawns on me, maybe he doesn't have to.

Wake up alone in our room, his side of the futon cool and smooth. My stomach writhes with hunger—one of the after-effects of Emptiness. Slip on my robe, open the translucent panels a crack, step out onto bare boards. The moon's low in the black sky. I tiptoe along, imagining leftover sushi, maybe a bowl of cold spicy tofu.

A loud belch stops me outside the shining panels. Followed by lusty slurping noises. Someone—Oro?—has had the same idea and is inhaling a big bowl of noodles. For once I will not be impulsive. The screens aren't quite closed. I put my eye to the crack. All the directors of Shiru Entertainment Conglomerate are there: Mr. Anaka, Mr. Shinoda, Mr. Naruse, Mr. Kobayashi, Mr. Arakawa. They suck at long bamboo straws. I follow the straws down. Oro lies on his back on the long red lacquer table, eyes opening, staring at nothing. The scar that runs down the center of his torso is open also, a gaping crimson mouth. The bamboo straws stir about in its depths, sucking up *shiru*.

What Hermiko said at the barbecue place in Roppongi a long time ago comes back to me: "All the people who grant him power ... he is their nourishment too."

Stumble back to my room. The works are in the box next to Oro's hard pillow. So is the glass tube, still about a third full of silver. I crawl under the low table that separates the futon from the sitting area. It feels safe—safer—wedged in like this, with a lid over me.

Emptiness. I feel like this time I deserve the full effect.

17

Under

It's often such an effort not to treat your body with
the contempt it deserves. The doctors and nurses
at the Smile Training Center in Kobe understood this, and
kept me lightly restrained and heavily sedated, like the
troubled pop stars, burned-out CEOs and scandal-plagued
politicians they were accustomed to treating.

I don't remember arriving there, never bothered to ask
who brought me. That world—*his* world—no longer concerned me. I was glad to be free of it, only sorry I wasn't
even more free. I do remember lying under the table, back
on Shodoshima, cloven needle before my eyes, the tentative, testing spurt of Emptiness into the air and then easing
it, oh, several times, into the bluest vein on the underside
of my left arm. In muscle it had been a rumble, then a quak-
ing, but in the vein it was the smooth night train, carrying
me away.

After the first day or so at Smile Training Center I wasn't
really in a coma, I just refused to open my eyes. There was
nothing I wanted to see, and what was said over my bed I

couldn't understand. This felt familiar, and just about right. I had nowhere to go, no special plans. Or rather, I had had a plan and it had failed. I was simply waiting for the next opportunity. Sometimes, when they left the door open, I could hear a man somewhere along the corridor incessantly calling out "Sony *kampai!*"

I don't know how long I had been there when the door slid open and rubber soles stamped across the tile floor. Small hands slapped my cheeks hard.

"Louise, Louise, wake up now please."

The voice was familiar but I couldn't place it. If I went back to sleep it would go away.

"Louise, I come for you. Wake up!" The bedsheet was whipped off me. I lay shivering in my hospital gown. I knew that voice. I opened one eye.

"Ha! You false sleeper, Louise." Camille Anaka, RN, stood at the side of my bed in a crisp nurse's uniform, matching cap and a six-strand pearl choker. Her chauffeur, also in hospital whites, stood behind her, a wheelchair parked at his side.

"Get up, quick-quick." Mrs. Anaka poked me in the ribs. "We sling you out."

"Bring," I quietly corrected her. "You bring me out."

The chauffeur untied my wrists and ankles and together they lifted me from the bed into the chair.

"Terrible, terrible," Mrs. Anaka whispered, plump hands massaging my shriveled wrists. "They treat you like animal."

We rolled along a dazzling corridor that made me close my eyes again. Other rubber soles slapped up to us and jabbered, but Mrs. Anaka held her own, shrilling and shouting till they dropped away. Electric doors sighed open. My face and body were so numb it took me a moment to understand the pinpricks on my cheeks and arms. Rain.

In the back of the Bentley Mrs. Anaka commanded me to lie back and open my eyes. "You look awful, Louise."

My mind formulated an appropriate reply but my tongue was indisposed.

She held up an eyedropper, blue liquid jumping in the narrow glass tube.

"We make you better before you know." She let blue drops fall into my eyes.

Blueness flowed through me. It was like being filled with the sea.

———

The sky looked familiar, gently arched and white-blue. White buildings streamed past, low mountains between them. Kyoto. We pulled up to the stubby dark glass rectangle with the silver square over the door, just off Imadegawa. Mouth Bank.

"Welcome home, Louise," Mrs. Anaka cooed as the chauffeur hauled me out of the back seat and tried to fold me into the wheelchair. But once he'd levered me upright I refused to sit down again. Mrs. Anaka signaled to him that it was all right. Moving behind me, she got a firm grip on my shoulders and pushed me through the revolving door and along the winding path, white gravel sharp and cool against my bare feet. We crossed over the Bridge of Lethe. Plum-colored carp, mouths agape, surveyed our slow passage. Through the segmented bamboo archway we floated like a pair of ghosts in a silent film, into the silver-doored elevator and down into the green glass corridors where you could see, if you chose, from room to room to room. I did not choose.

Mrs. Anaka led me to a transparent room next to the bath. About a million years ago she and Suki sponged me down there with fragrant oils. I would have asked how Suki was now, had I been a different, interested person. I think Mrs. Anaka picked this room because she thought the constant sound of sluicing water would calm me.

I lay down on the white pallet that was the room's only furnishing. Mrs. Anaka hovered over me, eyedropper in one hand. I took it from her and squeezed the blueness into my eyes.

—

Day and night are gone here. Through the walls I see many things. Sometimes I'm visited by boys from Lethbridge High. The most popular boys in the school, the ones who recognized me only after the sun went down. A row of them stand shirtless in the room on the left, jeans slowly sinking toward their cowboy boots, which are caked with manure and straw. They are as good as television, these boys—how they arch their backs and their knees and thighs tremble and buck, the way their eyes go black at the crucial moment. When the thick discharge rolls down the glass, I fall to my knees and lick the cool surface.

Later they come back naked and the glass becomes a membrane, thin and clammy as a surgeon's glove. They can feel me, finger me, enter me any way they like without the inconvenience of flesh on flesh.

You'd think by now I'd know to hang back. In the long run it only leaves me sad. But something compels me.

Nostalgia.

One day, one night, it occurs to me to try the door, see if I can force the lock. It isn't locked.

I begin to explore the corridors.

In the first room I enter a single book lies on a low red lacquer table. Vellum bound, title stamped in gold: *Anna Karenina*. It's exactly like the one I read as a teenager back in Canada, part of a series my father ordered up from the States.

The book falls open in my hands. Shiny white crumbs hide in the furrow between pages 214 and 215. I tease out a crumb, smell it: chocolate. I see myself gobbling down chunk after chunk of white chocolate while I devoured Anna and Vronsky. I place the morsel on my tongue. It tastes dusty-sweet, my mouth fills with saliva. From nowhere comes music, an old Beatles song, one I never liked. What's it called? "Norwegian Wood." The chocolate goes bitter in my mouth. I try to spit it out but only the taste is left. I run from the room.

Farther along the corridor I stare into a doorless cubicle bathed in red light. A surgeon's table draped in white. To one side, a tray laid with stainless steel surgical implements. Glad I can't get in there. My father was a reconstructive surgeon—perfected his technique during the Second World War. Later on, when I was a teenager, he painstakingly corrected my protuberant lips so that I would no longer resemble Eleanor Roosevelt, who I kind of liked.

Sometimes a man comes to sleep with me on my narrow pallet. I am always asleep when he arrives and I pretend to remain that way throughout his visit—I assume he prefers this too. He speaks to my sleeping eyes. "My name is Mr. Eguchi," he says the first time he comes. "I am full of the ugliness of age." I haven't yet known the ugliness of age but I have been acquainted with my own ugliness from the day I was born, so I feel comfortable with Mr. Eguchi. He brings with him the sound of distant crashing surf. I can feel him watch me sleep. When he thinks I am truly gone in dreams he draws back the quilt and suddenly the room fills with the sweet-sour milky smell of a nursing baby. He undoes the tie of my hospital gown and touches my breast softly with one finger as though he too is looking for milk. I'm sorry to disappoint him. The sound of waves breaking against a high cliff comes nearer. Old Mr. Eguchi puts his face to my breast and sucks. This we call the optimism of age. When at last he pulls his mouth away his lips are stained with blood. He licks them clean and says, "The aged have death, and the young have love, and death comes once, and love comes over and over again."

Mrs. Anaka is my only other visitor. At first she came frequently, dispensing comfort the only way she knew how. She touched me with practiced skill. When she had gone I felt cleaned-out inside. The outer me could have used a bath or just a hosing down, but all the water here is under glass. Her visits have become more widely spaced of late. She doesn't like it when I cry out too much.

In another room there is a wide meadow ringed by russet maples. My mother and father lie on a woolen army blanket. Over them my mother has drawn a tartan cashmere throw. My father lies on his back, the throw pulled up to his neck. From under the throw the barrel of a shotgun protrudes, touching the underside of his carefully shaved chin. My mother, curled on her side next to him, wipes his damp brow with a white handkerchief and whispers encouragement into his ear. No other sound comes from this room, that wide meadow—only my mother's whispers, my father's clacking teeth. There is a door but I will not open it.

The room I go to most is piled with suitcases. They look like my own. I don't need a door to enter this room: it is as if I never leave it. As the black taxi honks down in the street, I pack, unpack and repack this luggage which is not quite my own, unfurling lengths of multicolored cloth like a mad magician. Sleeves from absent sweaters, single moth-eaten trouser legs, the dangling straps of misplaced evening gowns, yellowed strips of elastic from panties and bras long since disintegrated. I can do this for hours, days, longer—arranging it all by color, size, texture, ruination. I fold and refold them neatly, stack them in tottering piles, secrete the best and the worst in the stretchy interior pockets of night cases and makeup cases and carry-ons. I never get it right, that's the continuing beauty of it. The horn honks down in the street and I have to start all over again—empty pockets and compartments, shift cases, unstack, unpack, unfold, re-fold fragments from clothes I couldn't wear even if they were whole.

Often through the fourth wall of the suitcase room a man and a boy watch me pack and unpack. Both Japanese. I can tell they are father and son by the distance between them. The father, in his thirties, wears black-framed spectacles. The left lens magnifies his eye so that it swims, dark fish in a bowl. The other lens is plain glass, the dead eye behind it like a knothole in a tree. He is running to fat and stinks of cigarettes and whiskey. The boy is different ages. Sometimes an infant with a squirming growth on his skull. Other times he is four or five, his smoothly shaved head as discolored as a bruised peach. Once or twice the boy is almost an adult. He makes music with his mouth but you wouldn't call it singing.

When he opens his mouth very wide I can see that other room, with the surgeon's table. A tray laid with a white cloth. On the tray four things: a pretty silver needle like the one in the fairy tale, a skein of black surgical thread, a long stainless steel hypodermic, a pair of translucent surgeon's gloves. When I was sixteen my father found out about the boys with shit-caked boots. He decided my other lips were a problem too. A scar would please him more than a gaping wound. My father was a very jealous man. But his needlework came to naught. A gangly sharp-toothed boy from the next valley bit the sutures in two even before the swelling had gone down. Me, I have always been on the side of the wound. My wound. Oro will have to take care of his own. That is what I call betrayal, passing yourself off as whole.

Bluetime.

———

How long has she been standing in the doorway? Her neat little cape hanging just so, precious wings on the heels of her Tragic Amusement running shoes.

"Go away!" I shout at her, except no words come out. A long time since I have bothered with a voice.

"Louise," she says, "I have looked and looked for you."

"Right here," I croak.

"I am sorry?" She gives me the big dark eyes, fluttering lashes and all.

"I've been right here all along."

She steps over the high threshold. If she comes near enough I'll knock the sincerity right off her face. "I have looked everywhere. Everyone was so concerned when you disappeared from Smile Training Center."

"Cut the crap, Hermiko. I didn't disappear—Mrs. Anaka brought me here."

Hermiko half bows and holds the pose, to better study the floor. "Mrs. Anaka acted without the knowledge or permission of Shiru Entertainment Conglomerate. It took us a long time to trace you here."

I think about this for a while. "I guess you're on the board?"

She reacts even more slowly than I speak. "The board?"

"You're on the board of directors of Shiru Entertainment Conglomerate."

She shakes her head and smiles becomingly. "Oh no, Louise, I am merely their messenger. I come with an offer. Don't you want to get out of here?"

I look about me, at the transparent green walls, at all the rooms receding into the distance in every direction, the constant sound of water as it pours down, the eyedropper shining on the floor beside my pallet. "That's the last thing on my mind."

"But you must …"

I reach for the eyedropper.

——

I come around, she's still here. She kneels beside my white pallet, whispering into my ear. "In your absence Oro's world became a calmer place. The Shiru directors were pleased. Suddenly he had more time to work and the desire to do nothing else. He poured all his grief, all his pain into the preparation of his new CD. He stopped sleeping, filled his nights writing song after song. Each one for you, Louise. From his Turtle a whole world of lament arose, in which all the world reappeared: forest and valley, road and town, field and stream and animal. Around his lament world, even as around the other earth, a sun revolved in a silent star-filled heaven, a lament heaven, with its own disfigured stars.

"When the CD came out, no one could bear to listen to it, the songs were so sad. Except for the boys. Kai and Kei, Reeves Steve, Yasujiro, Nagisa, Masahiro—they all put away their Judy Garland 78s and LPs and CDs and listened only to 3:02 *a.m. a Sunday in November*, for this was the CD's title and the exact time he found you, Louise, under the table at the Shodoshima villa with the hypodermic dangling from your arm.

"You understand that Oro has never had an unsuccessful *anything*. The Shiru directorate was concerned about the flat sales figures after the launch of 3:02 *a.m. a Sunday in November*, but not unduly so. They were sure that his upcoming concert tour would turn the tide, for they knew that no one could deliver a song, even a difficult painful one, the way Oro could. The first tour date, at his request, was at Peachblossom Festival Hall in Osaka. He asked me to attend. How could I refuse? Only half the seats had been sold.

"I was the only person in my row in the first balcony. There were no banners, no *son et lumière*. He didn't unravel like a mummy or slide down a steep staircase on his belly like a glittering snake. Instead he walked out onstage wearing a black shirt and gray trousers. He sat in a wooden folding chair, Turtle tucked under his arm. He and his instrument were inseparable now, as if it had grown into his left arm like a slip of golden roses grafted onto an olive tree. When he played it was clear he sang to someone but not to the audience. I could see his boys down in the front row, tears streaming down their cheeks. The rest of the audience left quickly, plush seats sighing shut behind them. The Oro tour moved on to Nagoya and closed there, failing to sell even a third of the available tickets."

Her voice is soft and yet insistent. But it has no power for me. I have constructed a world of my own too. Lament has no place in it. The air in this place carries nothing but the wind of forgetfulness.

—

Still here. I admire her persistence.

"He needs you, Louise."

"Shiru Entertainment Conglomerate needs me to stir up more gravy."

She is silent for a moment. "You were not always this hard."

"You were not always this false, Hermiko."

"In what way have I lied to you?"

Let me count the ways. And then suddenly I see my entire stay in Japan laid out before me as though it is a completed story, a play enacted again and again in one of the glass-walled rooms. The clarity astounds me. When has my life ever seemed so ordered or carefully patterned? Everyone appears at the exact appropriate time, each in a costume resplendent with meaning, from Mrs. Nakamura to the beautiful old lady, from Dr. Ho and his dancing needles to little Nobu pulling on his skinny white pud. Keiko and all the Little Ones scatter across the classroom in dervish imitation of a helicopter and Oro calls from the roof of my hotel, long coat cracking like a black sail in the night wind, whispering, "Hello, hello, hello."

Hermiko is right. No one has ever lied to me here, they all just assumed I knew my part.

I do now, even if I'm not clear about the ending.

Hermiko's eyes stare into mine. "You have reached a decision, Louise. I can see it."

"Not quite." I pick up the eyedropper. "How about a quick plunge in the ocean?" She tilts back her head and I let the drops fall like rain, first into her eyes, then into mine.

—

How she got me to my feet is a mystery. Maybe Mrs. Anaka helped. They even went to the trouble of dressing me. After a fashion. Strips of silk, elastic, wool, bandage, trail from my body. Keeping upright is the hard part. I focus on the wings of Hermiko's running shoes, the rest is automatic. We move along the curving corridors, my steps constricted by the cloth that festoons me. From time to time I stumble, but it is no bother. I am not impatient for the end. She pauses

while I bend to untangle a dragging sleeve, a length of wool
or elastic. Unwinding myself, I feel like I'm undressing a
child. I've gone so deep within myself—is this what preg-
nancy is like? To be filled with an emptiness, sweeter and
more vast than anything Oro can offer? This must be a pregnant woman's chastity too, my cunt has closed like a flower
at twilight. Don't need it any more. Beyond need now.

As we near the threshold to the other world, plum-
colored carp jostle at our feet. Hermiko touches my arm in
encouragement. It hurts, like an undesired kiss, reminds me
what the world is like. I almost turn around. But I want to
see how it ends. Just don't let anyone say, she went back
for love.

18

Nevers

"In the movie *Hiroshima mon amour*, the woman—I
wish I could remember her name—comes from a
town in France called Nevers. She is an actress, in Japan
to make a movie. She meets a Japanese man, an architect.
They have an affair, fall in love. He has a wife and children
who are away for the weekend or something. The actress
must return to France once her part in the movie—she plays
a nurse—is finished. For the role she wears a white Red
Cross kerchief in her blonde hair. The points where the
kerchief ties stand up like ears so she looks like a beautiful
cat. The nail polish she wears makes her nails shine like
obsidian."

"It is very sad," Michiko sighs for about the hundredth
time.

"Isn't it?" I say without feeling it. The more I try to re-
construct it the sillier the movie sounds. It seemed profound when I was at university but then a lot of things did
then. "In English it's what we call a doomed love."

"Doomed love," Keiko repeats, searching my eyes.

"Doomed love becomes a metaphor for war and death. The Frenchwoman, when she was young, fell in love with a German soldier. It was wartime, he was killed. When the war was over the people of Nevers shaved her head to humiliate her for falling in love with the enemy. Her parents locked her in the basement and she went mad for a time. Love with the Japanese man brings up memories of destruction and madness. He was away from Hiroshima when the bomb fell. He came back to the atomized place that had been his home. For both of them the past is too painful to remember, impossible to forget."

They're quieter, now I'm back. But then so am I. Not one of them has asked an awkward question, made a joke or a sly innuendo. No *"mokka-mokka-mokka."* Japanese tact cradles my heart. Nothing seems to have happened while I was away. My students look at me expectantly, eager to resume rehearsing for the end-of-term revue. Down the hall I can hear Madame Watanabe drilling Dirt Troupe through the more difficult passages of *The Birds.* (I think having them whistle "Bye Bye Blackbird" as a finale is probably a mistake, but who am I to interfere?) It's as if they've all been waiting for me. Now the show can go on.

"Let's run through the opening duet. Keiko, as an architect you are a little sleek and cold, like the modern buildings you design."

"Sleek?"

"Smooth, spotless, streamlined."

"What I wear?"

"Something very plain. Mrs. Yanagi in wardrobe is

taking care of everything. Dark trousers, white dress shirt, maybe a tie loosened at the collar."

Keiko gets up from her cushion. "Architect walk like this." She flows across the rehearsal room with the grace and assurance of a Japanese male who knows where he has been and where he's going. They may amount to the same thing but he takes pride in the fact that he owns them both.

"Very nice, Keiko. Michiko, you want to try the French actress?"

She shakes her head, eyes wet. "Not ready. I am sorry."

"Fumiko?"

Fumiko whispers something to Noriko, who giggles behind her hands.

I give Fumiko a photocopied sheet of the lyrics. "Noriko on piano?"

"OK." Noriko plops down on the piano stool, bangs out a few minor chords.

I clap my hands. "From the top."

"'You know nothing of my city,'" Keiko sings in a sturdy alto.

"'I felt the heat of Peace Square.'" Fumiko has a nice clear soprano. When she puts her hands over her face to ward off the heat it has the added advantage of hiding the mole.

"'You saw nothing.'" Keiko's so into it—nothing gestural about her performance. Anger and accusation surge like a current through her body.

"'I saw the news.'" Fumiko warbles on "news."

"'You invented it all.'" Somehow Keiko gets the sneer into the words but not on his lips.

"'I saw it all!'" I don't think Fumiko's quite right for the part. Too histrionic, like a kabuki Joan Crawford.

They join hands for the chorus: "'An entire city lifted off the ground, then raining down in ashes, on the seven streams of the River Ota.'"

———

This isn't going to work. Not the show. Me. Here. Back. People are far too kind, from my students down to the cafeteria ladies, who slip me extra portions of rice gruel. It is the elaborate kindness exhibited to those in mourning or to … can you be kind to the dead? I'm dead here, at the school, in Japan. Time for me to go. I'll finish the term, put on the show, of course. Then I'll be off.

It's always been like this. It's not that I don't see the patterns in my life, it's more that I'm helpless to correct them. I always do OK in a new place. People think I'm funny, unusual. That lasts until I've been around awhile. Then they get to know me and find out how unusual. When that happens there's nothing for it but to leave. I can't change who I am or what people see in me. It's probably not even a question of seeing. More like an odor. They can't help but smell the rot. I am lucky in this way: a fox can't smell its own tracks. At least that's what my father always claimed. And he should know.

So, finish the show, slip away. No point in telling Oro. He's happy to have me back. He must be the only one who doesn't smell anything at all. I spent the weekend at his place in Tokyo. On Sunday morning someone knocked at the door, he wanted me to hide under the breakfast table. It turned out to be one of his managers. I hid in the bathroom and made as much noise as I could, running the bath, splashing about, loudly humming. Sometimes I think this new arrangement is convenient for Oro. I am available but not apparent in his life. He writes songs of such happiness and contentment. His star has risen as high as it can go in this world. Nothing for me but invisibility. It's only the world of appearances you've lost, I tell myself. But that's the only world I've got.

The least I can do is go out with a bang.

—

It's not a real audience but Cocoon Hall is more than half full. All the troupes are here in force—Air, Fire, Water and Dirt—along with their swaggering TopStars. The cafeteria ladies, the guys from Compound Services who fixed my shoji screens, the ladies from wardrobe and makeup, the gauntleted assistants from Graceful Statement Design School, *including* a scowling Mr. Sasaki. He's here to watch me crash and burn. Mr. Arakawa is up in the royal box. The beautiful old lady sits behind him in a flame-colored kimono.

The twelve-piece orchestra in the pit strikes up a rather martial rendition of "Lullaby of Birdland." Madame Watanabe's girls go on first. I watch from the wings. The tallest apprentice member of Dirt Troupe wanders onstage wearing a chic sixties suit and a blonde wig piled atop her head like a ziggurat. She steps into a rowboat, takes a seat, picks up the oars. Strips of green and white satin ripple behind her. The orchestra goes quiet. I'll give Madame Watanabe one thing: it's a magnificent *coup de théâtre* when the first bird swoops down out of the flies like it's just escaped from a

German expressionist painting—cobalt breast, beating ocher wings, beak brilliant as orange peel. After that the *mise en scène* becomes a little bloody and overwrought, but still ... real imagination there.

—

During the interval I slip down to Sublevel B, where I've secreted Oro in a dressing room I hope Madame Watanabe knows nothing about. Mrs. Yanagi and two assistants flutter over him.

He smiles at me from the glass. "How do I look?"

"Perfect." The hair that shows under the Red Cross kerchief is blond, but ash blond, almost gray. The cross itself is a deep red, close to purple. His fingernails shine black, his skin's a shade paler than white.

"Isn't he beautiful?" Mrs. Yanagi beams in the glass, penguin earrings bobbing.

"Is everybody ready?" Oro says. He stands up and kisses me. I can't feel his tongue for thinking how I'm going to miss it.

Mrs. Yanagi and the two assistants applaud.

Out in the corridor he takes my hand and pulls me into one of the big rehearsal rooms. He fumbles for the dimmer switch, the lights come up low. I can see him in all the mirrors. A thousand-thousand Oros recede into infinity.

"There is something wrong." He touches his nose. "I can smell it."

I nod. "I can't live like this."

"Like what?"

"Living a shadow life with you."

"I know." He hangs his head in a most becoming way. Actors.

"It's time for me to leave."

"Leave?"

"Go back to where—" I start to laugh and can't stop for a while. "I was going to say, 'Go back to where I belong,' except there's no such place."

He looks at my face, a thousand-thousand faces, in the mirrors. "There is another way."

"Yeah?"

"You could come with me. I have gone as far as I can go here. It will always be another CD, another TV commercial, another hit movie. This has become so boring for me. Disgusting. I know only one thing, Louise. I want to be with you. But no more hiding. This world is too small, too tight."

"But where can we go?"

He stares at his own reflections now. "You can leave with me tonight."

"Sure. To a beach in Fiji?"

"A far better place than that."

"And how do we get there?"

His eyes fix on mine. "Through the darkness. A long sleep and a new awakening."

"Oh please, Oro—what movie is that from? I slept my fill at Smile Training Center and Mouth Bank."

From behind his black movie-star eyes something shines bright and deep, like an unknown constellation. "I am serious, Louise. This is the one thing I can give you, Louise—a life beyond life, changeless and unending. I can give you—"

Not the moment to laugh—I know that by now, when he's putting together a big dramatic speech—but I can't help myself. "Oro, give it a rest."

I don't know how he did it, but for an instant I see him in the mirrors as though underwater. And I can see myself there with him. Our faces float through the rippling dark. There is such peace.

"We'd better get going." I turn off the lights. Our reflections sink into darkness. "You don't want to miss your cue."

He stops at the threshold between dark room and bright hallway. "Remember, Louise, whatever happens, I will be with you always."

Music up and out.

We run for the elevator.

—

The girls wait nervously in the wings. Michiko looks like she has just thrown up. Only Keiko seems composed, until she glimpses Oro. One look in her eyes and I know her crush on me is over. She takes his ashen hands and brings them to her lips.

No overture for us. Instead a collage of sounds: cars honking, muted voices, the sound of a train rumbling into a cavernous station, a high female voice—Akiko's—announcing "Shin-Hiroshima." A blinding flash of light and the girls run onstage, somber in gray shrouds and mushroom-cloud hats.

At the last moment Keiko remembers to fold back the sleeves of her white dress shirt. She takes his hands and leads Oro onstage. He is so pretty in the bright lights, for a second I forget he's not a blonde Frenchwoman. I can hear murmurs from the audience. "'Hiroshima mon amour,'" the two of them sing, a cappella. "'Hiroshima mon amour,'" and the set slides in, a black-and-white street scene.

In the wings opposite me I can see Madame Watanabe huddled with her birds. Her mouth gapes, her eyes stare in disbelief. I can tell she's trying to figure out who our female lead is. Tippi Hedren runs up to her, blood still smeared across her forehead. She points to Oro and whispers in Madame Watanabe's ear.

"'You know nothing of Hiroshima,'" Keiko sings.

"'I felt the heat in Peace Square.'" Oro's voice is high and haunting as a child's.

"'You saw nothing.'" Keiko is in Oro's face now, hatred and passion twist her voice.

"'I saw tourists—'"

Madame Watanabe flies out onstage, the big German expressionist birds flutter and caw angrily behind her. "This is outrage," she cries. "This is desecration."

Mr. Arakawa and the beautiful old lady stand up in the royal box. For a moment, everyone freezes. Oro looks back over his shoulder at me. And smiles.

Madame Watanabe swoops down on him, rips off the Red Cross kerchief. The blond wig comes with it. He looks like a beautiful cat stripped of its fur.

"Defilement!" Madame Watanabe screams. "Man on Heartful Purity stage. Impure. Impure!" She spews out a lot of Japanese after that, in case anyone's missed the point.

Keiko shoves Madame Watanabe out of the way and takes Oro in her arms. Together they sing: "'An entire city lifted off the ground, then raining down in ashes, on the seven streams of the River Ota.'"

The birds are at them now, cawing, flashes of cobalt
and acid yellow. At first Keiko takes the worst of the pecking—she tries to shield Oro with her arms. The birds drive
them from the stage. Black feathers drift down into the pit.
The audience sits stunned. Michiko, Noriko, Fumiko and
the others wander about the stage under their mushroom-
cloud hats, whispering the refrain: "'Hiroshima mon amour,
Hiroshima mon amour.'" A girl from Air Troupe jumps up
from her seat and applauds wildly. Someone thinks to ring
down the curtain.

Exeunt omnes.

One Year Later

19

—

Shodoshima

Trying to get this place tidied up. I am a tidy-up person. The boys are a help, but they're so easily distracted. Except for Kai. He pads barefoot along the veranda, golden torso shining in the sun. The tatami mat he carries has a bit of gold-stamped border dangling from it.

"The main reception rooms," he announces, "are in apple-eye order. Kei and Nagisa and the others have gone into town to buy liquor and other necessities."

"That's good, Kai. It's 'apple-pie order,' by the way."

He laughs. "What was I thinking? Oh yes, 'apple of his eye,' 'apple-pie order.' My English is so unfortunate. What time will your friend be arriving?"

A sound from the garden. I turn my head and am quick enough to catch the great silver carp in mid-leap. "Bonnie? She's not really a friend, just someone I knew in another life. An American lady who does documentaries about Japan. You know, how lacquer is made, the indigo dye process, creative package tying."

He flicks a piece of fluff off the damaged tatami mat. "And who watches such films?"

"Got me, Kai."

"And now she makes a movie about you, Louise."

"About Oro."

"About both of you. It was his story but now you are the teller." He leans the panel against the wall. "It will be a big crew?"

"Bigger than Bonnie used to work with. She said there would be three production teams coming with her—one from PBS, one from Canal Plus in France and one from Channel 4 in England. Plus her regular crew."

"Why so many countries?" Kai asks.

"I guess this is usual for a co-production. The more countries involved, the bigger the budget. Ever since *Harikari Lovers* opened the Official Competition at Cannes last year there's been growing interest in Oro in France and throughout the West."

His gaze travels over the garden. "Do you think they'll want to film out here as well as in the house?"

"I'm sure they'll want to get the garden. So typically Japanese." I make a face and he grins at me. "They can run the opening titles over a slow pan of the pond or something."

"They could interview you in the main reception room," Kai suggests. "It gets the best light in the afternoon." He smiles, half-closing his eyes. "Perhaps they will want to film you in the bedroom also."

I turn to him. "The consort in her native habitat? Is all your stuff cleared out of there?"

He looks at me from under long lashes. "Guess what I found peeking out from under our futon?" He reaches into the back pocket of his cut-offs and pulls out a stretch of silver slink.

"Holy smokes, what's that?" It lightly clinks as he dangles it in front of my eyes.

"Steve Reeves's chain-mail posing strap." Kai giggles into his hands. "Remember the other night when Yasujiro made that big batch of mushroom chip cookies? Remember how Steve Reeves got all oiled up and climbed up on the table to—"

A silver-furred monkey swings down from the branches of an ornamental tree. "Hey, Shohei," I call out to him. He turns his back to give me a quick swing of vermilion testicles. Not unlike the dance Steve Reeves performed sometime after we finished the second platter of cookies. I can hear the other monkeys rustling in the bushes. Since I moved in, a bunch of them have migrated over from Wild Monkey Park to keep me company.

"I was also thinking we could take Bonnie up to Broken Tree Temple, show them where he stopped the earthquake with his song."

"Good idea," Kai says, "with the Inland Sea in the background. Do you think they'll want to shoot in the bathhouse?" He tries to lure Shohei onto the veranda with kissing noises.

"No one's to go anywhere near the bathhouse. I want the door locked. Now."

He picks up the tatami mat and hurries off.

I go into the main reception room to make sure everything's in order. In the niche at the far end I've hung the original cover art for Oro's last CD, a plain linen scroll with a black calligraphy square on it: □. The English title (it's gone platinum around the world) is *Way Out*.

The suitcases are neatly stacked in one corner. I lift the lid of one of them. Narrow strips of fabric spill out onto the tatami. We get a lot of visitors—Japanese and a growing number of *gaijin* too—most of them unannounced. They're on their way to Olive Island's eighty-ninth shrine: Broken Tree Temple. Inevitably they ask for something to remember Oro by. It was my idea to tear his wardrobe into strips so everyone can have a piece of him.

That's what happened when Madame Watanabe's birds got hold of him. Keiko survived the attack, although they don't think she'll ever regain full vision in her right eye. Funny thing, when I visited her in hospital she confessed that she was the donor of the gift cantaloupe. Keiko returned to Heartful Purity in the spring. Hermiko says she's shaping up to be their biggest TopStar ever.

Shohei creeps into the room. "It's OK, baby," I call to him. He joins me crouching in front of the biggest suitcase. Pulling out shreds of black velvet, silver lamé, gray silk, he proceeds to festoon himself.

When I get up at last he follows me along the veranda. Fabric trails off him like loosened bandages. Just want to make sure the bathhouse is properly secured.

I unlock the door and let it swing open. It takes my eyes a few seconds to adjust to the darkness of the fragrant room. Everything is as it should be. Kai is so reliable. Pretty easy

on the eyes too. No Oro, of course, but I don't need another
one. The lid is on the big sake barrel that he had converted
into a bath. A tray with a ceramic flagon and two lacquer
saucers sits on the top step of the staircase that curves up the
barrel's side. I sit down on the low bench that runs along the
east wall and look up at them.

When he asked me to go away with him that night in
the mirrored rehearsal hall, I thought he was kidding. I've
entertained a lot of propositions in my life, but no one had
ever offered immortality. Sometimes I wonder if I made the
right choice. Certain days it sounds inviting, to step away
from the world and all its changes and pain. Hauling up
buckets from beauty's well till it's bone dry. Evening bones,
shit and stench, chaos and putrescence. But like I said, I've
always been on the side of the wound. I like it here.

I've been a *gaijin* all my life. The beauty part of Japan
is that no one here has ever pretended I was anything but
foreign.

When it was all over and the journalists had gone and
the police had driven away, taking Madame Watanabe and
three Dirt Troupe girls with them, the beautiful old lady
came to my bungalow at Heartful Purity. She brought me
two gifts: the deed to this villa and Oro's head swaddled in
a length of silver brocade.

I keep it in the bath there. Sometimes, when the moon
is full, I come out here alone, press the button so the roof
retracts. The bright points of the Lyre—good old Turtle—
shine in the dark sky. I slide the lid off the bath and as the
moonlight spills in Oro opens his eyes and sings to me.

Acknowledgments

I would like to thank Louise Lundrigan, for lending me her name and other sterling attributes; Margaret and Richard Lock, for knowledge of Japan as profound as mine is shallow; Hiroshi Mikami, for being Hiroshi; Hiroshi Taguchi, for precious inside information; Geraldine Sherman and Donald Ritchie, for pointing the way to the Inland Sea; and Anne Carson, for everything.

My gratitude goes as well to the Canada Council for the Arts.

I am also indebted to many Japanese filmmakers and novelists, whose work introduced me to Japan long before I traveled there. Chapter 17—"Under"—in particular was heavily influenced by Yasunari Kawabata's *House of the Sleeping Beauties*, Kenzaburo Oë's *A Personal Matter* and Haruki Marukami's *Norwegian Wood*. Traces of Rainer Maria Rilke's "Orpheus, Eurydice, Hermes" can also be detected there.

My editor, Anne Collins, and my agent, Jennifer Barclay, shepherded this book through many changes, all of them for the better. For that no thanks are sufficient.